Trouble Maker

Also by Liliana Hart

Dirty Rotten Scoundrel
Down and Dirty

STANDALONE NOVELS/NOVELLAS
All About Eve
Paradise Disguised
Catch Me If You Can
Who's Riding Red?
Goldilocks and the Three Behrs
Strangers in the Night
Naughty or Nice

Trouble Maker
By Liliana Hart

A MacKenzie Family Novel

EVIL EYE
CONCEPTS

Trouble Maker
A MacKenzie Family Novel
Copyright 2016 Liliana Hart
ISBN: 978-1-942299-47-9

Published by Evil Eye Concepts, Incorporated

Acknowledgments

A huge thank you to M.J. Rose and Liz Berry for listening to me when I said I had a crazy idea. You never blinked and you saw all the possibilities. You guys are, as always, amazing and treasured friends.

Thanks to Christopher Rice, Cristin Harber, Avery Flynn, Robin Covington, and Kimberly Kincaid for agreeing to be part of this project. You guys are all exceptional and I'm so honored that you chose to explore the MacKenzie World.

Thanks to Jillian Stein for doing such an amazing job with social media and promo. You're the best!

And a huge thanks to my husband, Scott Silverii, for staying up with me until four in the morning while I finished this book. And also for providing me with Milk Duds and Route 44 iced tea. It's nice to surface from a book haze and see you're still there, plugging along with me. I love you more than you can imagine.

An Introduction to the MacKenzie Family World

Dear Readers,

I'm thrilled to be able to introduce the MacKenzie Family World to you. I asked five of my favorite authors to create their own characters and put them into the world you all know and love. These amazing authors revisited Surrender, Montana, and through their imagination you'll get to meet new characters, while reuniting with some of your favorites.

These stories are hot, hot, hot—exactly what you'd expect from a MacKenzie story—and it was pure pleasure for me to read each and every one of them and see my world through someone else's eyes. They definitely did the series justice, and I hope you discover five new authors to put on your auto-buy list.

Make sure you check out *Troublemaker,* a brand new, full-length MacKenzie novel written by me. And yes, you'll get to see more glimpses of Shane before his book comes out next year.

So grab a glass of wine, pour a bubble bath, and prepare to Surrender.

Love Always,

Liliana Hart

Available now!

Dedication

To Scott— Because you told me you loved my "winter body" and it made me laugh. I must really love you.

"Trouble is the next best thing to enjoyment; there is no fate in the world so horrible as to have no share in either its joy or sorrows."

~Henry Wordsworth Longfellow

Chapter One

Surrender, Montana
Fifteen Years Ago…

She'd seen her father's death.

Marnie Whitlock curled into a ball on the small twin bed and whimpered as pain shot through her body at the movement. The brutal heat of the day had carried into night, and there was no air conditioning in the small two-bedroom house she'd lived in her entire life. The old wooden window in her room was swollen with age, but she'd managed to raise it a few precious inches earlier that day. The breeze barely stirred the worn Priscillas hanging from the curtain rod.

She shivered under the thin, nubby sheet as fever crept through her body. She couldn't remember ever hurting as badly as she did in that moment. In one year and three days she'd taste freedom. She'd pack her bags and never set foot in Surrender, Montana, again.

Innocence was such a fragile thing. She hadn't been innocent since the age of four—since the first time he'd taken the tanned leather belt he wore like a religion around his waist and beat her bloody. Her mother had stood by helpless, wringing her hands and wondering if her turn was coming. But she never interfered or tried to protect her daughter from the vicious arcs of the belt.

Even at four years old, Marnie knew she'd done wrong. Daddy said she had the devil inside of her, and her mama always told her to watch what she said. It was her own fault she got the beating. Daddy didn't like hearing about it when she saw things that weren't right in front of her own eyes. And she'd been sassy on top of it because she'd asked how come there weren't any presents under the little Christmas tree someone had given them.

"My friend Darcy has lots of presents under her Christmas tree. How come we don't have any? You've got all that money just sitting in your glove box. You're supposed to provide. Mrs. Beasley said it's a man's duty to provide for his family. And Mama had to put back all those groceries when we were at the store yesterday because she didn't have enough money."

"Marnie," her mama whispered, appalled. She looked back and forth between her child and her husband. "We've got what we need. Don't sass your daddy."

"How do you know about the money in the glove box, Marnie?" Daddy asked.

His voice was real soft. Gentle even. He sat in the secondhand recliner and kept his eyes on the television.

Marnie looked at her mama, but she had her head down, focused on the dishes she was washing in the sink. But Marnie could see her hands were shaking.

"I saw it," Marnie said, clutching her nightgown with her fist.

"You went outside and saw it in my truck?"

She hesitated in answering and he turned his head to look at her—frigid blue eyes the color of a lake in winter.

"You were snooping through my truck?" he asked a different way.

"I just saw it," she said softly, her heart thudding in her chest. "Like in a dream." Her daddy was scary. But when he looked at her like that he was the scariest. She felt warmth dribble down her legs and to the floor as her bladder released. No one moved.

He stood up slowly and towered over her, and she heard her mother's whimper from the kitchen as she continued with the dishes.

"What else did you see?"

"I—I don't know," she stuttered out. "You were just playing cards. And then you took all the money and put it in the glove box. You drove into town and that lady was waiting for you on the steps. How come you kissed her but you never kiss Mama?"

That was the last question she asked before his belt swished through the loops—a long hiss and slither—and then the lightning crack of the whip as the belt landed across the middle of her back.

No—Daddy hadn't liked her saying those things at all.

Chapter Two

Thank God for the MacKenzies.

Marnie had learned through the years to keep her mouth shut and stay out of Harley Whitlock's way. The older she got, the further apart the beatings came. Mostly because she tried hard to stay out of the little clapboard house with the leaking roof and sagging porch, and at sixteen, she'd gotten very good at avoiding him.

She spent most of her afternoons and weekends at Darcy MacKenzie's house. They'd been thick as thieves since they'd been seated next to each other in Mrs. Green's kindergarten class. It was much easier to pretend she belonged to them—to a family that loved her unconditionally and didn't discipline with a leather strap and the smell of Jim Beam on their breath. To pretend the pretty blue-and-white room with the princess bed, and the closet full of clothes Darcy let her borrow so she wouldn't have to wear the same three shirts week after week, belonged to her.

Her daddy spent most of his days and nights down at Duffey's playing poker and drinking in the back room until Duffey tossed him and his buddies out. She assumed Daddy showed up at the MacKenzie Ranch for work from time to time, because they hadn't been kicked out of the house they rented from James and Mary MacKenzie, and he always seemed to have money for his drinks and the poker pot.

Her father hated her. She knew that. But he also feared her gift. He'd said more than once that the devil lived inside of her and beating it out was the only way to get cleansed. She'd believed him when she was younger, but as she'd gotten older she'd started doing research. There were others like her. They might not have a gift as strong as hers, but she wasn't alone.

She was also smart enough to know her days of living under the same roof as Harley Whitlock were numbered. But something had gotten into her tonight. Maybe it *was* the devil after all. Because she hadn't cared about his anger or the belt. Even doormats had a threshold of tolerance before they unraveled.

Carson Hamilton owned a large patch of land on the outskirts of town, and every year he loaned it out to a traveling carnival. In they came with their trailers and tents and rides, setting up within a matter of hours. And when the sun went down, the whirl and flash of carnival lights could be seen all over Surrender. Even from their little house down in the valley.

Marnie had borrowed some of her freedom money from the Mason jar she kept hidden beneath the pieces of tin and rotten wood from a shed that had fallen down in their backyard. It had only taken her once to see her room ransacked and the money she'd kept in her drawer gone before she'd found a better hiding place.

Darcy had told her she was making an investment in herself. So Marnie had splurged to buy mascara and a lip-gloss that Darcy had sworn plumped her lips right up. Of course, her daddy would kill her if he ever saw her wearing makeup. They were tools of the devil, used to incite boys, and only sluts and actresses wore makeup.

Marnie had taken a little more of her freedom money so she could buy a Coke and cotton candy and still have enough to purchase tickets for a few rides. She'd been saving the last year, ever since she'd been old enough to get a part-time job at the library. And by her calculations, in one year and three days, she'd have enough saved so she could move to the city and find a better job while she went to college.

She'd ridden with Mama to the fairgrounds and helped her unload some homemade jams and a quilt that would be sold at the auction. Anything to bring in a little more money.

Marnie thought her mama had probably been beautiful once. Helen Whitlock was too thin and worry had etched deep lines around her mouth and eyes. There was no extra money for haircuts or color, so her dark hair was long and streaked with gray. She almost always wore it pulled straight back off her face in a tight bun. At thirty-eight, she should've still looked youthful and healthy, but instead she looked like an old, mousy woman, afraid of her own shadow.

Mama chose to stay in the tent with all the other women and the goods, so that left Marnie alone and to her own devices. She knew Darcy was around somewhere, so she set out to find her. What she found instead was Beckett Hamilton.

Her heart fluttered in her chest at the sight of him. He was nineteen and home for the summer after his first year of college. She couldn't remember a time when she hadn't loved him, even when she was a little girl and she and Darcy would spy on her brothers and Beckett. The boys almost always had better adventures than they did. Mostly because they were boys and they had the run of the ranch. But there'd always been something about Beckett that captivated her attention. He was quiet, but there was a presence about him that made the others listen when he spoke.

He was king of the land—the heir to one of the wealthiest ranches in the country—and he was so far out of her league she should've been ashamed of even dreaming that he could love her in return. He was a little over six feet in height, and she'd noticed after his time away at college that he'd come back a little broader in the shoulders and chest. His hair was sandy blond and thick and wavy, always a little bit messy, and his eyes were storm cloud gray. She'd always thought it odd that there were no other variations of color in his eyes. Just gray. But they were direct and there was kindness in them. And when he smiled his eyes smiled too.

Beckett was surrounded by Declan, Shane, Thomas, and Riley MacKenzie. Declan and Shane were brothers, Thomas and Riley were brothers, and their respective fathers were brothers. They were all close to the same age. Shane was the youngest at eighteen and a senior at Surrender High School. Riley was the oldest at twenty-two and finishing up college. The others fell in between. And more often than not, they could be found hanging out together.

Beckett stood with a pellet gun to his shoulder, knocking down wooden ducks with little pings. He'd always had eyes like a hawk. The MacKenzies hooted with laughter as Beckett was handed the oversized stuffed bear as a prize, but the grin on his face was wide with pride.

Darcy came running up at that point, black hair flying and cheeks flushed with color. The heat had curled little tendrils around her face and neck, and the short denim skirt and crop top she wore showed off curves Marnie envied. Darcy dragged Emmitt Strain behind her, and he was holding a couple of small stuffed animals and a bag of popcorn.

"Man, that was awesome, Beck," Darcy said. "I couldn't see the whole thing because Shane's giant head was in the way. But you really mowed down those helpless wooden ducks."

"Shut up, Darce," Shane said. His eyes narrowed as he looked down at Darcy and Emmitt's joined hands, and Emmitt paled and quickly let go when he saw the look on Shane's face.

Marnie almost smiled. She already knew there was no hope for Darcy and Emmitt. Emmitt played defense for the football team, but he didn't have much of a spine outside of the football field. Or a brain. Darcy had both and she was destined for someone she couldn't walk all over.

Darcy had always accepted Marnie's gift, and she'd never shared the things Marnie had told her in confidence. They were the very best of friends, and they'd shared many secrets—crushes and gossip they'd heard from their parents or around town—but not everything. Darcy suspected about her father—it was impossible not to when it sometimes took days for Marnie to recover so she could be seen in public—but though Darcy's eyes asked unspoken questions, Marnie had never confided in her. It was a shame she kept to herself.

Marnie often got clear visions of the people she was closest to, and she'd had several of Darcy. She'd understood at an early age that the gift she'd been given wasn't always meant to share. That altering people's decisions could change the entire course of their lives. The responsibility was one she didn't take lightly. And drawing attention to herself was the last thing she wanted. Her father had gotten a call once from a center in Denver, wanting to put her through a series of tests, but he hadn't been interested since they weren't willing to pay. He'd beaten her for that too. Because she was useless and couldn't pay her own way.

But she continued to see things. And she continued to keep those things to herself. But sometimes…sometimes the loneliness of her gift was overwhelming. She knew she could trust Darcy, and in one of those moments of loneliness Marnie let it slip that Darcy had already met her future husband. Darcy hadn't been surprised by the news. But she said until Brant Scott got some sense in his head, she could at least have a little fun making him suffer.

Marnie stood to the outside of the group, observing the easy way the MacKenzies were with each other. They'd never made her feel less, despite the fact that their families owned the ranches her daddy worked for, but she wasn't like them. It couldn't have been more obvious. They didn't know what it was like to go hungry because there wasn't enough money to put food on the table. Daddy teased her about being the rich kids' trash, but she never felt that way. Or hardly ever.

"I've been looking all over for you, Marnie," Darcy said. "Mama said you could spend the night if you want and she'll make pancakes in the morning. Cade's home for a little while and he said he'd put up a new swing over the lake so we can jump in. And maybe we can go to the movies tomorrow night. That new Julia Roberts movie is playing if you want to see it, though I'd rather watch Bruce Willis blow up things. But Emmitt will have to buy our tickets because it's rated R."

"God, do you ever shut up?" Shane asked.

"No, and this is an A-B conversation. C you later."

Marnie looked back and forth between the siblings and decided to jump in before they started arguing. MacKenzie arguments had been known to last weeks.

"I'm sure Mama won't mind," Marnie said. "It'll give us a chance to study for our chemistry final too."

Darcy's eyes widened with great drama and she put her hands on Marnie's shoulders, shaking her gently. "When are you going to start listening to me? Live a little, woman. You'll ace that test no problem. We're in our prime." She held her arms open and spun around, and then she fluttered her eyelashes and flashed a sassy smile before putting her hands on her hips. "We've got the rest of our lives for all that serious stuff. It's time to have fun."

"Very responsible, Darce," Declan said to his sister. "Thank

God you've got Marnie to balance you out. I can only imagine the hellion you'd be without her."

"She's already a hellion," Riley piped up. "She'd be a monster."

Darcy turned on her cousin. "Shut up, Riley. Maybe you need to remember what I saw in the barn last week and that you owe me *big time.*"

The images in Darcy's head broadcast through Marnie's mind and the blood rushed to her cheeks in embarrassment. Riley was lying square on top of Colleen Walton and they were both naked as jaybirds. His bare buttocks flexed and Colleen's nails clawed into his back while she howled like a wet cat. Marnie didn't know a lot about sex, but Colleen was either in a lot of pain or she was enjoying herself immensely.

"Darcy…" Riley warned, his eyes narrowing with warning.

"Hey," she said, shrugging. "I'm the one that's probably going to need therapy. I'm just saying maybe you need to be a little nicer to me." Her grin was mischievous, but Darcy had always been good at holding her own against her brothers and cousins. As the only girl in the pack, she said it was her duty to give them hell.

"Come on, Dec," Riley said, slapping his cousin on the back. "Let's go grab a pizza and a beer. I've got better things to do than hang out with children."

Since Riley and Declan were the only two old enough to drink, it was a definite insult to the others.

"I don't know if I'd call Colleen Walton something better to do," Shane said snidely, elbowing Thomas in the ribs. "It's hard to tell the difference between her and a screech owl. You ever notice how every time you bring her to the house, the horses and cattle try to run into the barn and hide?"

"Or maybe they're trying to get a front row seat," Thomas sneered. "Everybody knows y'all go in there to—"

"Thomas!" Riley took a step forward and raised his fist and everyone took a step back. The MacKenzies fought more often than not, but to Marnie's trained eye it wasn't out of anger, like with her father. They seemed to enjoy fighting. As if it were a sport.

Beckett moved so he stood between the two before fists could start flying. "This isn't the place for a fight," he said. "You'll be hauled out by your ears before you get started. And watch what you're saying in front of the girls. Mrs. MacKenzie would skin you good if she heard you talk that way."

That was probably the only threat that could keep them in check. Mary MacKenzie was a force to be reckoned with when it came to keeping her boys in line—and that included her nephews too since their mother had passed on.

Riley nodded and took a step back. And then he grinned and gave Thomas and Shane a one-finger salute before he and Declan disappeared into the crowd.

Marnie had never thought about sex until the dreams started creeping in on her at night—Beckett's face and his lips as he kissed her in the dark—only to be interrupted by the snap of her father's belt as he punished her for having impure thoughts. Even her dreams were terrorized by her father.

Marnie could feel the heat in her cheeks at their candid talk, but she tried her best to act like it was no big deal. The truth was, she was scared to death of sex, and most of what she'd learned about it she and Darcy had overheard by listening in on her brothers. Her father had always said whores were the only ones who enjoyed sex, but Darcy said that was a flat-out lie and that she was going to enjoy the hell out of sex when she was ready to have it.

Darcy had talked her into borrowing the white cotton shorts and red top that stopped just above the top button of her shorts. It hung off one shoulder a little, showing the thin strap of the white tank she wore. She hadn't been brave enough to go without it as Darcy had suggested. She'd never felt comfortable showing much skin, but she had to admit the bold contrast of the colors showed off the tan she had been working on by laying out at the lake.

Her dark hair was thick and long and she'd braided it over one shoulder. Her eyes were dark and enhanced by the mascara she'd bought, though Darcy said it wasn't fair how she hardly needed it, and that women would kill for lashes like hers. Her lip-gloss had in fact plumped up her lips and they stung just a little bit. But she felt pretty and normal and a little more grown up. She could never hope to fill out the outfit like Darcy, so the shorts bagged on her just a little, but they were still finer than anything she owned.

"Marnie," Darcy said, getting her attention again. "Let's head over to the House of Horrors before the line gets too long. I saw Justin Appleby on the way over here. He'll ride it with you. He likes you."

"You're barking up the wrong tree there, Darce," Shane warned. "He likes to watch the guys shower in the locker room. Emmitt can back me up on that one."

Emmitt shrugged and looked at Darcy apologetically, not denying Shane's claim.

"Why can't you go away? You ruin everything," Darcy complained, pouting a little. "I swear I'm going to find your adoption papers and prove that you're not really one of us."

Marnie smiled. Darcy and Shane could've been twins, so similar was their appearance—black hair and piercing blue eyes shared by only a few of the MacKenzies. Not to mention identical smiles that could charm their way out of any kind of trouble.

Bells and whistles went off from the games around them as the crowd increased in size. Someone jostled her from behind and she was pushed off balance. She felt a solid wall meet her shoulder and a hand came up to steady her. She looked up into clear gray eyes and watched the dimple flutter in Beckett's left cheek as he smiled at her.

"Hello, Marnie," he whispered close to her ear so only she could hear. "I've always wondered what you'd feel like in my arms."

Chapter Three

Her breath caught as the heat from his fingers penetrated her skin and sizzled across her nerve endings like electric currents. Sound and movement stopped. It was only Beckett and the blood rushing in her ears.

And for a split second, her eyesight dimmed and she saw—felt—the softness of the quilt beneath her back and the fullness of the moon as it shone between the branches of the trees above her. The weight of him as he pressed her into the blanket. The feel of his bare skin against hers and the slickness of their skin as their bodies moved together in perfect harmony. Her heart thudded in her chest as his lips took hers in a passionate kiss and her body arched against his as stars exploded behind her eyes.

Sound whooshed back and she sucked in a deep breath. He was looking at her oddly and no wonder. There was no telling how long she'd been standing there blank-faced and unresponsive.

Darcy called it her "ramblings." When a vision overtook her and there was nothing she could do to control it. Sometimes they lasted for seconds. Sometimes several minutes. But there was no bringing her back from them once she was entrenched in the vision. It was when she was at her most vulnerable.

She couldn't explain her gift. It was just part of who she was. And it had taken her a long time to realize that not everyone could do what she could do and that she made people nervous. It was easy enough to see everyday thoughts or get strong images if she focused—especially if she physically touched the person she was trying to read. But the visions were different. They slammed into her like a Mack truck and left her helpless where she stood. They were powerful, and what she saw almost always came to pass—unless some odd hand of fate turned things in another direction.

What she'd seen had been as real as anything she'd ever experienced. Beckett would be her lover. And they'd find pleasure in each other. Joy burst in her heart. This wasn't like the hopeful imaginings she'd had in the darkness of her bedroom. This was reality that would come to pass. There'd been love between them—at least the beginnings of it—in the vision she saw.

"Are you okay?" he asked.

"I'm sorry," she stammered. "I didn't mean to bump into you."

"Relax," he said, as if he were soothing a frightened mare. "Like I said, I like how you feel in my arms." His smile was easy and disarming, but there was something in his eyes that was different than before. Or maybe she'd never noticed. Her body thrummed from the erotic vision and they were still speaking only to each other, the outside world ceasing to exist.

His gaze lingered on her bare shoulder and then moved up, so he was staring at her lips. His hand lingered on her arm, and she was glad she'd taken Darcy's advice and spruced herself up a little.

For one night, she was normal. She was like the other girls. There was no worry over whether or not there'd be a roof over her head by the end of the week. No worry over how they'd put food on the table. No worry that she'd washed and worn the same clothes more than once in a week. She was like Cinderella at the ball and she hoped that midnight never came.

The taste of that small amount of freedom went to her head and made her dizzy with elation.

"Hello? Earth to Beckett and Marnie," Darcy said, waving her arms near their faces.

Beckett smiled and looked at Darcy. "I heard you, Darcy. I just didn't want to be interrupted."

Marnie jerked her head in Darcy's direction, coming out of her stupor. She noticed that Shane and Thomas had wandered back over to the pellet guns, where they were engaged in a battle of who could kill the most wooden ducks.

"What I was saying," Darcy said good-naturedly, "was that you should take Marnie on the Ferris wheel. She likes it, but heights make me want to barf. Emmitt and I are going to try out the Tunnel of Love." Darcy wagged her eyebrows and winked at Emmitt.

To say that Darcy was a handful was an understatement. She was wild and full of adventure, but she had a heart as big as the ocean. She also wasn't the least bit afraid of heights, and Marnie shook her head at her friend. Darcy wasn't known for being subtle.

"Your brothers are going to kill you if you go into the Tunnel of Love and they find out about it," Beckett said.

"I guess you'd better not tell them then," she said cheekily. "I know how much you love me. You'd miss me if I were gone."

"You're right," Beckett said, and then he looked at Emmitt. "Which is why I'm comfortable telling Emmitt here to keep his hands to himself so the police don't have to hunt for his body parts. The MacKenzies are protective of their sister."

Emmitt swallowed and nodded frantically, and Darcy rolled her eyes and looked at Emmitt in disgust. It didn't take a vision for Marnie to see that Emmitt would be flying solo before the night was through.

"Don't put Beckett on the spot, Darcy," Marnie finally said, and then she turned to face Beckett. "There's no need to keep me company if you've got other things to do. I don't mind being on my own."

"I like Ferris wheels," he said. "When you get to the top you can see all of Surrender. I'd like to show you."

A riot of emotions sizzled through her body. Before the vision it had only been her imagination. She hadn't known what it felt like to be kissed. She hadn't known what it felt like to be pressed body-to-body, skin-to-skin. But the vision had given her a small glimpse of ecstasy, and being with him now was a mix between ultimate pleasure and pure torture. And she agreed with Darcy. When the time came to have sex she was going to enjoy the hell out of it. The little rebellion against her father made her giddy with anticipation. She'd take her freedom in small doses until the next year and three days was over.

"What do you say?" he asked, holding out his hand.

She smiled and placed her hand in his. She couldn't imagine a night ever being more perfect than this one. Darcy winked at her as Beckett led her away, and nervous anticipation had butterflies dancing in her stomach. She wanted to remember every detail—every sight and sound. She wanted to be able to recall every precious moment once she was alone. She could do that. Bring back sights and sounds and tastes once she'd experienced them.

His hand felt good in hers—right—and he didn't seem to mind that anyone could see them. Her shoulders straightened proudly as classmates took notice. She'd never been noticed before. She always flew right under the radar, especially when she stood next to Darcy. Marnie didn't mind it, and she didn't begrudge the attention given to her beautiful friend. In fact, she preferred to go unnoticed. Going unnoticed meant no one asked questions about her family, how she got that bruise on her collarbone, or why she'd had to miss a week of school while she let the bruises heal.

"Those must be some deep thoughts," Beckett said, smiling down at her. "Is everything okay?"

She forced away the thoughts that had clouded her mind and smiled. "Sorry, I was just letting my mind wander."

They got into the line for the Ferris wheel, but their hands stayed joined. Beckett held the teddy bear he'd won under his other arm. A little girl with pretty blonde pigtails, each one adorned with a big white bow, walked by, and he handed over the teddy bear, much to the girl's delight.

Beckett used his tickets for both of them and handed them over to an older man with a cigarette hanging out of his mouth. The attendant held the metal bar back for them and she slid into the seat first. The seats weren't large, so when Beckett scooted in beside her they were pressed thigh to thigh. If possible, her heart thudded faster in her chest and heat infused her body. And then the car jerked as they began their ascent.

The space was confined, so he raised his arm and put it across the back of the seat. His fingers toyed absently with the strap of her tank top and she looked straight ahead as they rose higher and higher, praying he'd never stop.

"Whenever I see you and Darcy together it always seems like you've got plenty to say."

"You make me nervous," she said.

"I've been told I have that affect on people," he said soberly. "You might be more nervous to know I'm not all that fond of heights and if I pass out you should just ignore it and pretend I was manly and tough for the duration of the ride."

Marnie laughed. "I'll do my best to pretend. As long as you don't throw up on me or pass out in my lap."

"I'm a gentleman," he said. "I'll make sure to pass out in the opposite direction. College has taught me well."

"Do you miss it?" she blurted out. "Your friends there, I mean?" And then she closed her eyes and wished she could fall into a hole. Could she have asked a more stupid question?

"Nope, not at all. It's a necessary evil," he said, shrugging. "The ranch is in my blood. I'd rather be there working and getting my hands dirty than sitting in a classroom. But it's going to be mine one day and I've got to learn how to keep it profitable and expand it in any way I can. It's my legacy."

Marnie thought about that for a moment and wondered what that might feel like—to have a legacy. Once she graduated from high school she'd be on her own. Starting a new life with a new beginning.

"You're destined for it," she said softly. "You'll sit through the classes and the lectures because you love what will one day be yours. Even though you hate your statistics professor."

His grin widened. "Hey, how'd you know? That's cool. There have always been rumors you could read people's minds. Wish I could do it, though it's probably like Spiderman. With great power comes great responsibility. I'm not sure I'd have that kind of control. My mother said men don't start making good decisions until they're close to fifty. And she said when they're with other men that they never make good decisions, so it's probably best you're the one with the powers."

She forced a smile, but felt the blood drain from her face. She'd completely let down her guard.

"No, sorry to disappoint you," she stuttered out. "I—I must've overheard it somewhere. Maybe from Darcy."

He looked at her skeptically. "It's okay, you know. We've been in and out of each other's pockets for a lot of years now. I'd have to be completely clueless not to notice you're a little…different…than other girls. There was that time you practically threw a fit to keep all of us home that day we wanted to go to the lake. We ditched you and Darcy to play hide-and-seek out in the barn. We were so mad at you."

Her smile was sad as she looked out over Surrender. There was so much land out there, so much world. She spent a lot of time living in those other worlds in her head, just to escape.

"We didn't find out until that night that a big tree had fallen in the lake and washed downstream with the current, taking three kids with it. It took the search and rescue team two days to find their bodies. That could've been us. Except you saved us."

"Three people still died." She hadn't been able to see that there would be other deaths. Her gift was selective.

"You can't save everyone. That's a burden no one should bear."

The butterflies in her stomach turned to boulders and she closed her eyes as the breeze ruffled her hair and cooled the sweat on her skin.

"Rumors are usually just that," she finally said, wanting nothing more than to put her feet on solid ground again. "You should know by now you can't believe everything you hear. Especially in Surrender."

"Marnie," he said softly.

She turned to face him, only to realize too late how close he was. Inches separated them and her gaze locked with his. The Ferris wheel had stopped just shy of the highest point, and the lights from the other rides flashed shadows across his face.

"You can always trust me," he whispered.

She felt his words against her lips. Her palms dampened and her stomach flipped. And then his lips touched hers and her eyelids fluttered closed. Colors of every hue exploded behind her eyelids and her pulse raced.

She'd felt his touch during the brief vision she'd had—but nothing could compare to the reality of his lips against her. The softness. The tingle that spread to her very core. Her first kiss—and it far surpassed any expectation or dream.

When they broke apart, Marnie's heart was racing and she stared at him with equal parts shock and wonder. She saw just a glimpse into Beckett's mind before she gained control and left him his privacy. But it was enough to know that he'd been just as affected as she had, and that he was determined to take things slow. Very slow. He cared about her. About her feelings and that she was inexperienced. It was enough of a glimpse to realize that she'd have to be the one to move things to the next stage. He was giving her control.

Her lips felt swollen and tingly. And then she realized the car had come to a stop and they were back at the bottom where they'd started, and the attendant was unhooking the latch to let them out.

Beckett helped her down the steps and she was surprised to realize her legs were unsteady. She didn't have any words—anything to say to fill the gaps—and she felt completely out of her element. If she were like some other girls she might be able to smile or flirt or laugh, but there was only a soul-quenching knowledge that something had changed irrevocably in her life.

"I've wanted to do that for a long time," Beckett said solemnly. He took her hand and led her to the other side of the fairgrounds, toward the barricades that had been erected to divide the carnival from the makeshift parking lot they'd set up in another part of the grassy field. The lot was scattered with cars and the area was empty of people.

She couldn't lie to him. Not with her feelings so close to the surface. "I've wanted you to do that for a long time," she admitted. "Why'd you wait so long?"

He grinned and said, "I could never tell if you liked me. You're always so serious. But every once in a while, I'd see you out of the corner of my eye—those big brown eyes watching me closely—and then you'd look away if I turned. But the blush across your cheeks let me know that maybe you were thinking of me like I was thinking of you."

"It just always seemed so impossible," she said, not denying his observations. "You're away at school, and I'm—" She was going to say nobody, but she caught herself before the word could leave her mouth.

"It's Surrender. The separation is only temporary," he said. "We can make this work. We've got the whole summer before I've got to go back to school. And next year when you leave for college maybe you'll find a place where the distance isn't so bad."

She could see the excitement in his eyes. Beckett was a planner. It came with ranch life. You always thought ahead to the next season and what needed to be accomplished.

The smile slowly left her face as she realized her future was not one that could include Beckett. Not even for a short while. It wasn't fair to him. She had to escape her father. And there was no Surrender in her future.

The vision she'd had earlier flashed through her mind once more. The way they lay entangled on a blanket beneath the stars, their naked bodies sliding together with familiarity. Her cry of pleasure and his shout of triumph as the ecstasy built to a peak. And then it fizzled like a candle at the end of its wick.

"Beckett," she whispered sadly, her hand coming up to touch his face.

And then he leaned down and kissed her again. This time was just as sweet, and the taste of him went straight to her head. His lips became bolder and she felt his tongue slip into her mouth. Her hands moved from his face to the back of his neck and she pressed against him, enjoying the new sensations of his body against hers.

"Marnie!" a familiar voice sounded in the distance.

She jerked back as if she'd been doused with cold water and looked around frantically, searching for that voice that always struck fear into her heart. Her first thought was to push Beckett behind her. Her daddy would kill him.

"You need to go right now," she said to Beckett. "Go and don't look back."

"I'm an adult, Marnie. I can take responsibility for my actions," he said, trying to soothe her. "He's got every right to be upset. You're his daughter."

She caught sight of him just past the barricade, standing next to his old pickup truck, the red tip of his cigarette hanging out of his mouth. Harley didn't look upset. He looked murderous.

"Marnie, you fucking slut," he yelled. "You get over here now. If I have to come get you you'll regret it."

Embarrassment heated her cheeks at the way her father spoke. "You don't understand," she said to Beckett, pushing him back another step. "He'll kill you. Just go before you make things worse."

Beckett stopped and stared at her—a long, slow, dissecting stare that made her feel too exposed.

"Just go, please," she begged.

"How long has this been going on? Jesus, does Darcy know? Why hasn't anyone done anything?"

"Because it's nobody's business. Besides, who's going to do anything about it?" she asked, the resentment she'd felt her whole life sneaking out. "My own mother would back him up. Sometimes the only thing to do is survive until you can escape."

"I'm not going to leave you alone. Is there somewhere you can go? To the MacKenzie's?"

"There's no point. He'd just hurt them too." There was no point being angry at Beckett. He was just trying to help. "I know how to deal with him."

"I'm not leaving you," he repeated. "We'll deal with him together."

Harley stood in front of his truck and the lights from the carnival cast eerie shadows across his body. He was a big man—you had to be to tackle steers or get bulls to cooperate—and his hair was sandy and thin on top. He flicked his cigarette onto the ground and didn't bother stamping it out.

Before she could protest further, Beckett took her hand and pulled her straight into the Lion's Den.

"You're the Hamilton boy," Harley said as they approached.

She could smell the whiskey on him from where she stood. It wasn't like him to be in a crowded place like the fair. Once Duffey kicked him out of the bar he almost always went home to sleep it off. But something about this time was different.

"Yes, sir. I am," Beckett answered warily. He'd smelled the whiskey too and caution eased into his voice. "I was just about to take Marnie home. My car is just over there."

"Don't lie to me, boy," Harley spat. "You think because she spreads her legs for you that you have some kind of right to her? I'm sure all the boys feel the same way. She's always been wicked. That girl's got the devil inside of her. Nothing but trouble and a burden to her mama and me."

Marnie stayed silent. It never did any good to argue, and it was the same speech she'd heard hundreds of times.

"That seems doubtful, sir," Beckett said. "Like I said, I was just going to take her home."

Harley smiled and fear snaked down Marnie's spine. "Run back to your daddy, boy. She's not worth the fight, no matter how good the pussy is. They never are." He chuckled and Marnie felt Beckett go stiff with anger next to her. "Get in the car, girl. I won't tell you a second time."

She let go of Beckett's hand and started to move forward, but he grabbed her wrist. "He's been drinking," Beckett said. "It's not safe to go with him."

"He's always drinking. And it's a lot safer to go with him now and just deal with it than to defy him," she hissed. "Do what he says. He'll hurt you, and I can't have that on my conscience. He'll sleep it off and won't remember any of this by morning."

"And what about you?" Beckett asked. "Will you be fine?"

"Sure," she said. "I always am."

"I'm going to get the sheriff. This is fucking insane, Marnie. He can't get away with this. And I won't let him hurt you."

"One year and three days," she said, pulling out of his grasp.

"What's that?" he asked.

"Freedom." She took a step forward to face her destiny and the world went black as the vision took over. It was powerful. And violent. Her knees buckled and she went down to the ground in a smooth motion. Everything around her stopped—sight and sound—and all she could see was the scene unfolding before her.

Her father sitting in the backroom at Duffey's like he had so many times before. The three other men at the table giving each other wary glances as Harley became more intoxicated. He was losing. And he was angry about it. Then Mitch Jones laid down three aces and Harley's temper exploded. He accused Mitch of cheating and then swiped his arm across the table, clearing cards and poker chips and money. There was no stopping him. Harley was a freight train of rage and injustice. And he picked up the heavy wooden chair and slammed it into Mitch's face. Then he did it again. And again.

"You killed him," Marnie sobbed with horror. "The sheriff is looking for you. He's coming. You thought you could hide in the crowd, but he's coming for you. They'll all be looking for you.

You'll be surrounded."

"Son of a bitch," Harley said, kicking the front tire of his pickup truck. "Leave it to Mitch to go and die after a little tap on the head. Get in the truck. You're coming with me. I'll need a little insurance to get out of here."

"No, I'm not going," she said, scrambling to her feet. Beckett helped steady her and pushed her behind him. "They're coming for you." Panic tinged her voice. She could see better now that her eyes had adjusted to the darkness. The spatters of dried blood across his shirt and on the tip of his boot from where he'd kicked Mitch.

She'd forgotten how fast he was for a big man. There was no time to run into the safety of the crowd. Harley was in front of them in the blink of an eye. His fist connected with Beckett's stomach hard enough to double him over. And then he jerked her by the arm and tossed her over his shoulder in one smooth motion. She felt the liquid pop as her shoulder came out of joint and her scream was muffled against his back.

"Let her go," she heard Beckett say, his breath wheezing as he stood straight again. Then she heard the familiar sound of her father's fist hitting flesh. Beckett shared Harley's height, but at nineteen, he didn't have the strength or build of the other man.

"Stop it! Don't hurt him!" she yelled. She tasted the salt of her tears, but crying never did any good. Crying made it worse.

"Shut up, little bitch," Harley snarled. And then he tightened his grip around the back of her legs and marched toward his truck. She looked up in time to see a small crowd gathering and Beckett sprawled on the grass—unmoving. The door of the truck opened and she was tossed inside, her head hitting the center console with a sharp crack. Her vision went blurry for a split second and when she was able to focus again she saw an open bottle of Jim Beam in the cup holder.

Marnie scrambled to a sitting position as her father got in the cab of the pickup and she scooted as close to the door as she could. He turned the key in the ignition and it started up smoothly, and then he threw the truck in reverse and sped out of the grassy field, fishtailing onto the gravel road that led back into town.

He cut through back roads and across open land, checking the rearview mirror for anyone on his trail. There was no one. Just her.

"I need money," he said. "I know you've got a stash. Tramp like you probably makes decent cash whoring. You're going to give it to me or I'm going to gut you with my filet knife."

Marnie closed her eyes and tried to remember to breathe, but the fear was thick and cloying and it crawled across her skin like a toxic ooze. All she knew was she'd rather be dead than give up the one chance she had for freedom.

"I—I don't know what you're talking about," she stuttered.

She didn't even have time to flinch as the back of his hand connected with her cheek. Pain exploded along her jaw, and she tasted the coppery tang of blood as it filled her mouth. She pushed herself farther in the corner of the cab and looked at the door handle. She'd have to be fast to open the door and roll out into the street.

"Don't bother lying," he said. "You managed to tart yourself up with that makeup on your face. You got it and those slutty clothes from somewhere, so I know you got money. No wonder boys like that Hamilton kid are sniffing around. It's girls like you he'll fuck on the side while his respectable wife is home where she ought to be."

Her hand crept up the door until it was just inches from the handle.

"I'll break every one of those goddamned fingers if you try to open that door. Where's the money?" he asked again. And then he hit her in the ribs as an afterthought, though the angle was wrong so it wasn't as big of an impact as it could've been.

He laughed and the sound was pure evil. "I forgot I owed you that one. Only the devil could've told you about Mitch cheating at cards. I just wanted justice. And look at you, spouting filth and lies instead of defending me. Your mama and I would've done better to put you in a bag and drown you when you were born. Least you could do is make us rich. Worthless bitch."

They were still a couple miles away from the house and he was flying down the one-lane path, so gravel was pinging against the side of the truck. He slammed on the brakes and they skidded several feet before ending up inches shy of the big oak tree that sat in the middle of the fork in the road. The left side of the fork was MacKenzie land, and the little house they rented was along that path. The right side of the fork was Hamilton land.

Her heart thudded in her chest and sweat dampened the back of her shirt and shorts. Her hair had come loose and her mouth was swollen and split from where he'd hit her.

She was just plain tired. There was no winning this game her father played. There was no reason to fight back. To argue. But sometimes she thought about it. Because maybe if she fought back he'd go ahead and kill her.

He was out of the truck in a flash and around to her side, jerking open the passenger door. He pulled her out by the hair and threw her to the ground. She caught herself with her good arm and whimpered as her other shoulder throbbed. And then she heard the sound she'd dreaded almost every day of her life. The swish of leather as it was pulled through his belt loops.

"I don't like repeating myself, girl. I asked for money. And you're going to tell me where it is. What's yours is mine. I've provided you with shelter and food. And you owe me. Where is it?"

This first snap of the belt stung against her shoulders and she huddled into herself for protection, her face pressed against the dirt beneath the tree. Through every beating, every disappointment, every hardship, she'd kept her pride. She never begged for him to stop. She just rode it out and went to the place inside her head that kept her from going insane with the pain. Her focus was getting out. Escaping. And her freedom money was the only way to do that. She'd be damned if she'd hand it over to a monster.

She lost track of the number of times the belt whistled down across her back. Or the number of times he yelled, "Tell me, bitch!" But she knew the only way to save herself was to use the gift she'd been given. Even if it was a lie.

"He's coming," she croaked out, but he didn't hear her over his rage. So she took the chance and lifted her head so she could look right at him. "He's coming. The sheriff is on his way, and there are cars following him with angry men. They're going to drag you off to jail where you deserve to be."

He stopped and stared at her, sweat covering his face and dampening his clothes. The belt was slack down by his side. His breaths were heavy and his cold blue eyes were mean.

"Get up," he said. "And look me in the eye and say it. I don't hear no sirens. I think you're lyin'.'"

Marnie wasn't sure where she found the strength to get to her feet, but she did. She needed to be more convincing. Blood dripped down her back and into the waistband of her shorts and shivers wracked her body. And then something took over her. Defiance and rage and everything she hated about the man who'd created her.

Her voice wasn't recognizable as she spoke. But it held strength and power, and the vision washed over her with such clarity she almost wept in relief. She saw the end with a mighty force that gave her the strength to go on.

"They are coming for you, and they will find you," she said without inflection. "But they will not find you as you are now. I see your end. Your death is near, and it comes with screams of horror and flames. There will be no escape. Only the slow and torturous slide into death. And then hell awaits you. Run now. Maybe you can escape your fate."

He stared at her with fear in his eyes and he lifted the belt once more, but she didn't flinch. Didn't move. Then he turned and walked back to the truck, got inside, threw it in reverse, and drove away.

Two miles she walked. Until her body burned with fever and her feet developed blisters. She stood in front of the ramshackle house in the flood plain of the valley, the white paint peeling and the yard overgrown with weeds. The lights were out, and if the moon hadn't been full it would've been impossible to see anything.

But she put one foot in front of the other until she was inside. She moved through the house on autopilot, keeping the lights off. Her face throbbed. Her body was a mess, but she couldn't stomach the thought of standing long enough to take a shower.

She peeled the bloody top from her back, weeping as the dried patches pulled and tore her flesh. She discarded the shorts and shoes and stole one of her father's oversized undershirts from the basket of folded laundry on the table. He wouldn't be needing it. And then she gingerly crawled into bed and curled into a ball as the tears continued to fall.

Marnie lay huddled in the dark and waited for her father to die.

Chapter Four

Sometimes the visions crept in like fog across the water. But usually they slapped her with the force of a hurricane.

Pain and fever had lulled her to sleep, but when the vision came it appeared with such clarity that she felt his every thought and movement, as if she were an extension of his body.

The truck smelled of whiskey-soaked sweat, and his hands gripped the wheel like a vise so they wouldn't shake. His heart raced and fear had a stranglehold on him as he sped along the two-lane road toward the mountains. He was more afraid of her words than the cops catching him. Sheriff Rafferty was old and slow, and he'd spent too many years sitting behind a desk with his feet propped up. Besides, if Rafferty tried to take him in he could just kill him. One more body wouldn't make a difference.

Harley knew the roads like the back of his hand, and the moon was bright enough he didn't even need to turn on his headlights. They'd never catch him. He'd be over the mountains and across the border into Canada by the time they got their thumb out of their asses long enough to put out an alert for him.

But Helen was going to be a problem. He turned his head to look at his wife. Stupid bitch couldn't live without him. Didn't have the skills to live on her own, and damned if she hadn't been waiting for him with her rattletrap car parked so it blocked the street, waving her hands to get him to stop.

He didn't know how she'd found him, but he guessed she probably knew his habits better than most. She'd never been dumb, just worthless. Though he'd appreciated the money she'd earned from selling her jams and quilts at the carnival. It wasn't much, but added to the money he'd taken from the pot after Mitch had had the poor sense to die, he could live for a few days until he could steal some more or find another poker game.

But Helen was a liability, and she'd only slow him down. He decided to kill her with the same nonchalant shrug one might have when choosing ham or turkey on their sandwich. She sat beside him, twisting her hands nervously in her lap. She didn't ask what he'd done or why he was leaving. She would've heard the rumblings while she was at the fair. The old biddies in town knew things almost as soon as they'd happened. But Helen was a loyal lapdog and she'd served her purpose. He'd wait to kill her until they were in the mountains. The animals would get her before anyone would be able to find her body.

Harley turned on the radio to fill the silence, rapidly skipping through the channels since most of them were static. He came across a station that was mostly clear and then took a swig from the bottle of Jim Beam in the cup holder. He was going to wait a little while for a drink so his head could clear, but Helen was driving him crazy with her silent judgment. He didn't know if he could wait until they were in the mountains to kill her. Stupid bitch.

Even in the vision Marnie was amazed that he never once thought of her. Of what he'd done or how he'd left her. She was nothing to him. He truly didn't care if she lived or died.

The farther he drove the more irritated he became, until his mouth formed a snarl and sweat dripped from his temples. And then he heard the alert on the radio. They gave his name and a description of his truck. Then they said he was wanted for murder and considered highly dangerous. He almost grinned at that. Of course he was fucking dangerous. Nobody messed with Harley Whitlock. Just ask old Mitch.

He pressed down on the accelerator a little harder. It wouldn't be long until they got to the narrow one-way road that led to the mountain pass. The smile on his face was unnatural— anticipatory—for the only thought in his mind was seeing the surprise on Helen's face when he bashed her in the face with a rock.

He'd liked the surprise on Mitch's face when he'd hit him that first time. It made him chuckle just thinking about it, and he shook his head and sped a little faster. You could never recapture that first look of surprise. After the first time it was only screams and fear and begging. Though that held its own kind of appeal.

God, why wouldn't she shut up? The little whimpers escaping her thin, pinched lips were driving him fucking crazy. His hand shot out and he backhanded her across the mouth. And then he laughed. Nobody could touch him.

They drove another hour and the heater in the old truck couldn't keep up with the rapidly dropping temperatures. There was still snow up in the mountains. It was a good place to leave a body, and just the thought of what was coming made him hard with anticipation. Hell, maybe he'd give the old ball and chain one last go for old time's sake. Pussy was pussy. And he'd been going through a dry spell ever since that bitch Lavina had decided he'd been a little too rough with her.

How was he supposed to know she'd pass out? Lavina liked it rough just like he did, and boy, did she always go crazy writhing underneath him when he put his hands around her neck and squeezed. It made him shoot off like a rocket every time. But Lavina had been like all the other bitches out there. Begging for it and then crying foul like she hadn't wanted it in the first place.

He was rock hard and ready after thinking of that last time with Lavina and decided the least he could do was give Helen a little farewell fuck so her last moments would be enjoyable. That's the kind of thoughtful man he was. Always thinking of others.

He laughed again and fought the urge to just pull over and rut like a deer in mating season. It was all in the timing.

"We're going to stop up here and take a little break," he said, glancing at Helen. Her face was bloody and a little bruised, but he didn't mind that. He didn't have to look at her face. Wasn't much to look at anyway. But she had a nice round ass that he could plow into and her tits weren't so bad either.

The excitement had him accelerating toward the next curve, but it was sharper than he remembered. By the time he pumped the brake and turned the wheel, it was too late. The truck skidded and fishtailed before falling over the side of the mountain.

Marnie cried out in her sleep as the truck cleared a path

through the trees down the side of the mountain. They hit a boulder at the edge of the ravine and her father hit his head on the steering wheel. Her mother was already dead. Killed with the first impact. But drunk drivers were numbed by the alcohol and usually didn't know what was happening until someone was pulling them from the wreckage.

But not this time. Marnie smelled the gasoline and heard the hiss of the engine. Blood from the wound on his head dripped into his eyes and his hands were unsteady as he reached for the door handle. But it wouldn't open.

The soft whoosh of flames from beneath the hood spread quickly, and she felt the first sober panic penetrate his brain. He was going to die. And then he thought of her and the last words she'd spoken to him, and he knew his fate had been foretold. He died screaming, trapped in the flames.

When Marnie woke the next morning she was in the tub, her back and buttocks aching and the wounds crusted with blood. The trickle from the shower head dripped a steady beat on her thighs— her voice was hoarse. And all she could feel was relief.

He was dead.

Chapter Five

Present Day
Surrender, Montana

"Beckett Hamilton! I've got something to say to you."

Beckett stopped in his tracks and closed his eyes, praying the shrill voice that was the equivalent of nails scraping across a chalkboard was a figment of his imagination.

"Are you listenin' to me?"

Not a figment of his imagination. He should've listened to his father when he'd warned him to stay clear of town. Women were nothing but trouble. And this one was more trouble than most.

He'd been up since before dawn with his father at the barn. They'd been culling cows that weren't fertile to sell off, and administering vaccinations to the ones that were pregnant or still had breeding potential. After that, he'd ridden out to the hayfield to check on a baler that was acting up, and while he'd been out there he'd noticed a section of fence had fallen down. Life was never boring at Big Sky Ranch.

He'd already put in a full day and it was barely noon. His muscles ached and a fine layer of dust coated his clothes. He wouldn't have it any other way. But he'd gotten cocky. A good day's work and a crisp, clear day, and he'd decided he'd have lunch in town with Thomas and Riley MacKenzie.

It had been at least a month since he'd thought of Hazel Trout—maybe six weeks. They'd only seen each other a handful of times and a majority of that handful was spent naked. It was when she had her clothes on and her mouth open that he decided he'd better nip things in the bud before she got the wrong idea. But apparently he hadn't started nipping soon enough.

He'd always gone out of his way to make sure he parted on good terms with his lovers. Sure, some of them were hoping for more, but he always made it clear from the start that he had no intention of settling down any time soon. The ranch had become his life, especially since his father had retired two years ago and put everything in his hands, and there was no room for anything but the occasional good time.

But Hazel had been more persistent than most. And she hadn't been at all interested in parting as friends or on good terms. He hated that it had come to that, but like his father said, it was his own piss-poor fault for thinking with his dick instead of the brain the good Lord had given him. Hazel wasn't the kind of woman that would be satisfied with anything less than catching herself a cattleman. And a cattleman with money was even better. Beckett filled both those shoes.

For the last month she'd called and called. And when he'd stopped answering the phone, she'd resorted to leaving messages. They'd started out sweet, but by the time she was done his ears had been ringing. He hadn't even bothered to listen to the last dozen or so she'd left. She'd been sighted driving past the ranch a time or two, but there was a gate that led up to the main house and he'd made sure it was closed at all times.

But dammit, he refused to be held prisoner on his own land. He hadn't done anything wrong. The sooner they could bury the hatchet the sooner he could stop looking over his shoulder every time he stepped foot outside his house.

So he'd accepted the invitation from Riley for lunch and he'd driven his work truck into town, parking behind the sheriff's office. The sky was cloudless and the sun was a bright orange ball directly overhead. Fall had taken hold with a mighty grasp and the leaves had changed and were now falling to the ground. It would only be a week or two before the first frost, but it was nice out so he decided to leave his shearling jacket in the truck. His flannel shirt would be sufficient. He'd adjusted his ball cap and pocketed his keys, not bothering to lock the doors, and headed toward the diner.

There wasn't much to downtown Surrender. It had been erected in the late 1800s, and not much had changed since, other than the occasional shift of store ownership. The street was bricked and a little longer than a football field, and identical two-story wooden buildings that shared common brick walls lined both sides. They'd all been painted white, and black awnings covered the wooden sidewalks. Gas lanterns hung to the left side of each door and black letterboxes hung on the right.

The sheriff's office was located at the end of the street directly across from the bakery, and Cooper MacKenzie was near the end of his second term as sheriff. Cooper kept crime low and the occasional skirmish between neighboring ranches to a minimum, so there was no doubt he'd run unopposed again in the next election. Surrender wasn't exactly a hotbed of crime.

Next to the sheriff's office was a separate structure with long front steps that led up to massive columns and heavy wooden oak doors. Once upon a time, it had been the largest bank in the territory, but as towns began getting their own banks there wasn't a need for it anymore and the space went to waste. The people of Surrender weren't fond of change, but they also weren't fond of tearing down historic buildings, so it was turned into a library.

Beckett was halfway across the street when he heard Hazel yell out. Pedestrian traffic in town stopped as everyone's eyes turned toward the latest entertainment. When she called out a second time, he had no choice but to acknowledge that he'd heard her.

He turned around slowly and plastered an easygoing grin on his face. She'd followed him out into the street and stood at the opposite end so they faced each other like gunslingers.

Looking at her now, he wasn't sure what he'd ever seen in her. She was a pretty girl—or would've been if bitterness and anger hadn't etched itself permanently on her face—but she was still in her early twenties and immature with it. She was petite and trim and blonde, which had been his type for the past fifteen years. His luck with brunettes had run out the day Marnie had left town. And he could appreciate the way Hazel filled out the jeans and red sweater she wore. But looks only went so far.

"You're a goddamned liar, Beckett Hamilton," she yelled from down the street.

His eyebrows rose at her language and he could see crowds growing on each side of the street as customers and shop owners came outside to watch.

"Watch your language, Hazel. There might be children in earshot. Why don't we go inside and talk about this like adults?"

"You'd like that wouldn't you, mister high and mighty Hamilton." She dashed a tear off her cheek and then planted both fists on her hips. "I've been trying to talk to you for weeks, and you just ignore me. Well, I'm tired of being ignored. I'm gonna say what I have to say, and I'm going to do it right here."

"If that's the way you want to do it, then get it done. You're giving everyone their entertainment for the evening, and you'll be lucky if your mama doesn't wash your mouth out with soap after hearing about your language. I said what I had to say to you weeks ago. We had some good times together. Nothing more. I told you from the start I'm not ready to settle down, and I've got no interest in a serious relationship. So if you've got something to add to that then let's get this over with. I've got hay to bale this afternoon and I have no intention of being the center of the town's gossip today."

"Too late!" someone called out from the sidewalk. There was a smattering of chuckles, and he could see Thomas and Riley standing in front of the diner, arms crossed and smiling like loons. They were going to give him hell when this was over.

"You can't tell me we didn't have something special," Hazel called out. "We could've made a life together. I would've given you everything if you'd let me." She sniffled and her empowered speech was turning into a whine. "I believed in you. You said you loved me."

"Oh, no," Beckett said, reaching his limit. "Those words never crossed my lips. I'm sorry that you thought you could change my mind, but I was up-front with you from the beginning. I won't be pressured into anything."

"I'm pregnant," she yelled out, finding her mad again.

"Hazel, you and I both know that's a bald-faced lie."

"How do you know? We had sex, didn't we? Accidents happen." She looked entirely too smug.

"Then you head over to the doctor and bring me the results of the pregnancy test. And of course, we'll do a paternity test as well."

She gasped, the insult clear. "How dare you insinuate that I sleep around."

"It's been more than long enough for you to find someone else to try and rope and wrangle. I wasn't born yesterday and I know how these things work. If you were pregnant you would've known before today and would've been throwing it in my face and telling anyone who would listen. You've got marriage on the mind and I'm not biting. And you're only embarrassing yourself and your family by doing this. So if you want to play out this farce, go get your test done and come back and see me."

If looks could kill he'd already be six feet under. "I'm glad you've shown your true colors before I was saddled for a lifetime with you."

"There you go. Always look on the bright side."

She turned sharply on her heel and marched toward her car. Beckett sighed and ignored the curious stares of onlookers as he made his way toward Riley and Thomas.

"Shut up," he said before either of them could open their mouths to speak.

"Hey, man," Riley said, holding up his hands. "We're innocent. Don't take it out on us. Thomas will buy your lunch and make you feel better."

The diner was a throwback to another era. The floor was black-and-white squares of linoleum. The counter was long, and a freshly baked pie sat in a glass dome at the end. Red vinyl barstools sat like soldiers in front of the counter. Booths lined the perimeter of the diner and the seats were covered in the same red vinyl.

Gladys Dubois and her husband Milt had opened the diner just after their marriage more than fifty years before. Gladys had been seventeen at the time and Milt closer to thirty, and they figured if people were going to gossip about them anyway then they might as well give them a place to do it. Gladys had the disposition of a drill sergeant with hemorrhoids, and she still worked the front counter and waited tables. Her hair was flame red and added at least an extra foot to her height, and her lipstick bled into the wrinkles around her mouth.

Milt had worked the grill back in the kitchen, but he'd passed on about a decade before, so Gladys had hired Snoopy Gaines to flip hamburger patties and his wife Cori to handle the rest of the menu. Business had gone up a lot since Cori started working her magic in the kitchen. No one could make better fried chicken anywhere in the state.

"You've sure gotten yourself in a pickle, Beckett Hamilton," Gladys said from behind the counter. She was working a crossword puzzle and dividing her attention between that and the soap opera on the TV in the corner.

"No, ma'am," he said back, wishing once again he would've listened to his father and just stayed home. "I think I got my point across."

She cackled and slapped her bony hand on the counter. "Boy, you don't know nothin' about women. You mark my words, she's not ready to give up yet. I guarantee she had the wedding reception booked and a dress picked out. A woman doesn't go to that much trouble to quit after being rejected."

"She can book whatever she wants as long as she understands she'll have to knock me unconscious to get me to the church. Besides, in another month we're going to be right in the thick of calving season. Out of sight, out of mind. She'll forget all about me and find some other poor single sap."

Gladys shook her head. "I never realized you were so dumb. Good thing she's lying about that pregnancy. Oldest trick in the book. Between the two of you that baby wouldn't have had a prayer."

"Thank you, Gladys. I appreciate that. But there are plenty of single men left in Surrender."

"Honey, when you get to be my age everyone is either dead or everything droops so low they're not worth looking at without their clothes on." She turned her attention to Riley and Thomas. "You tell that cousin of yours to come see me and I'll give him some fried chicken on the house. Not a woman in this town would turn that man away from her bed, even without a leg. I could show him a thing or two."

"We'll let him know," Thomas said, the look on his face somewhere between amusement and horror.

They made their way to a corner booth and Thomas and Riley

stopped along the way to say hi to Danny Patterson and Lane Greyson, two of the deputies that worked for their brother Cooper.

Beckett slid in so his back was to the wall and checked his phone. It had been buzzing constantly since his little showdown with Hazel. He winced at the thought. He hated being the center of anyone's attention, not to mention the fact that he didn't like airing his dirty laundry. He'd always been private and discreet when it came to his relationships.

The diner was filling up fast, and heads turned and looked his way before going about their business. A couple walked in that immediately caught Beckett's attention. The man was tall and built like a truck. His blond hair was cut close to the scalp and he looked military. And dangerous. The woman with him was young and pretty and so city she might as well have been wearing a sign on her back. She had the body of a pinup, and her hair was long and black. Every eye in the place moved from looking at him to them. Thank God.

Thomas groaned and looked at the military guy. "Dammit, Devon, why can't I get rid of you? You're everywhere I turn."

"I guess I'm just your cross to bear. That's what you get for marrying my sister."

"Which should tell you how much I love that woman. When are you leaving again?"

"Kylie and I are on our way out, and we'll be out of your hair. But don't worry. I'll be back for Christmas."

"Good. I was worried you wouldn't make it," Thomas said dryly.

Devon grinned and then the two men shook hands.

"Y'all have a safe trip," Thomas said, and then he and Riley slid into the booth across from Beckett.

"My brother-in-law," Thomas said by way of explanation. "He's a new fixture in our lives and takes a little getting used to."

"Hell, he's the least of our problems," Riley said. "I'm more concerned about what Gladys is planning on teaching Shane. I can't decide whether to tell him to keep hiding in his house or convince him to come out just so I can watch Gladys put the moves on him." He shuddered and then lowered his voice to a whisper. "And I hate to admit it, but as soon as she said what she did I imagined her naked with Shane strapped to her bed. I'm going to have to go to therapy to erase that one."

Thomas laughed out loud and Beckett grinned at the thought of Riley laid out on a couch trying to describe that little fantasy.

Shane MacKenzie had been a Navy SEAL commander, but he'd been on leave and back home at the MacKenzie compound when an enemy had shown up on their doorstep, endangering the whole family. Shane had managed to save his sister-in-law, but the explosion had taken one of his legs and badly damaged the other. It was fortunate Thomas, who was a doctor, had been close by, otherwise Shane probably would've died.

It was something none of the MacKenzies liked to talk about because they all felt helpless when it came to Shane. He'd gone from a decorated soldier who'd commanded others to losing his leg and career in one fell swoop. He wasn't adjusting well. And they were all concerned for him.

"You're sick, man," Thomas said. "And that's saying something. Because now it's in my head and I blame you. I'm going to punch you later as compensation for the trauma."

"You haven't been able to punch me since you were fifteen."

"That's not true. I got in a doozy a couple of Christmases ago. You just didn't notice because you were on the bottom of the dog pile."

"That was you?" Riley asked, his eyes narrowed. "I had a black eye for almost two weeks."

"It's nice to see some things never change," Beckett said. "Though I'm surprised your wives let you get away with stuff like that anymore. Y'all have kids."

"Hell, are you kidding?" Riley asked. "They're the ones betting money on it. Aunt Mary usually ends it by turning the hose on everyone."

"If you think Aunt Mary's bad, what do you think *your* mother is going to do when she hears about this stunt Hazel tried to pull?" Thomas asked.

As if by some magical mother's intuition, Beckett's cell phone started to buzz on the table. He let it ring.

"I almost feel sorry for Hazel," Riley said. "You know how bad Judy's been wanting a grandchild. She even offered to be an honorary grandmother to our kids since you won't do your duty. Your mama's got a vicious streak. She'll probably let the air out of Hazel's tires for giving her false hope."

"Are you kidding?" Beckett said. "She's been jumping for joy ever since we stopped seeing each other. It's been almost two months and Mom still gives me a thumbs up whenever she sees me." Beckett shook his head and they took a break to order their drinks and food. The waitress was one he'd never seen before, but she didn't seem to mind Gladys's gruffness. She seemed very efficient, though it was hard to miss the baby bump growing under her apron.

He waited until their drinks were served before finishing the story. "I think the straw that broke the camel's back was when Hazel stopped by the house one day while Mom was there. Then Hazel proceeded to tell her how precious she looked and that she really carried off the look well despite her age."

Riley and Thomas gave identical dumbfounded looks and Beckett grinned at the memory. "If Mom had been holding a butcher knife you'd have gotten a phone call to come help me hide the body. I've never seen her so mad."

"Is that why you broke up?" Thomas asked.

"No, I broke up with her because she's never read a book. Or watched anything other than reality TV. I don't know who the Kardashians are. I don't know why she kept talking about them or why I should care. I'm sure she'll make someone a fine wife someday. Thank Christ it isn't going to be me."

"She'll figure it out soon enough," Thomas said, shrugging the matter off. "I'm more interested to hear what your thoughts are on the newest business moving into town. Have you seen her yet?"

"What business? Seen who?"

Riley's eyebrows almost went to his hairline in surprise. He slapped Thomas on the shoulder and grinned wide. "I can't believe you haven't heard. Judy is losing her touch."

"I haven't seen my mother in almost a week. I've been neck deep in pregnant cows, vaccines, and broken balers. What the hell are you talking about?"

"The little photography studio moving in next door to the sheriff's office. Where that fancy cake decorating place was that tried to put the bakery out of business. Didn't last two months with their high prices and snooty cakes."

"Cat's already talking about getting an appointment for us to get family photos taken," Thomas said, referring to his wife.

"I hope she dresses you and the kids in matching sailor outfits," Beckett said deadpan. "Now maybe one of you will explain why I should care about a photography studio. I'm sure it'll do a great business. It's smart of whoever put it in."

Thomas's smirk was identical to his brother's. "That's what we're trying to tell you. Marnie Whitlock is back in town. It's her place. She showed up last week out of nowhere and offered Aunt Mary and Uncle James full market value if they'd sell her the little house she and her family lived in. They tore that place down after Marnie went with social services. Harley would never let them do repairs on the house so it eventually became uninhabitable."

Beckett hadn't moved since the moment Thomas had said Marnie's name. His body felt like lead, and his brain was slow to process the news. In fact, everything seemed to be moving in slow motion. He could see Thomas's lips moving, but he couldn't hear the words. Only the blood rushing through his head and the sound of his heartbeat rabbiting in his chest.

He'd thought about Marnie every day after she'd left. Then as the years passed he thought of her every other day. And then it lessened to a couple of times a week as life got busy. But he still thought of her. The last he'd heard she was living in Savannah, Georgia, and had made quite a name for herself.

She'd been his first love. It had been wonder and fascination and innocence, and who knows if it would've lasted, but she'd had his complete focus from the moment he'd come home from college that summer until her life went to hell. He hadn't had the guts to tell her then. She'd taken his breath away, and he'd wondered why it had taken him so long to notice.

He'd come home from college feeling a little out of place in his parents' home, wondering how things had changed so drastically. How *he'd* changed. And then he caught a glimpse of Marnie while he was visiting the MacKenzies one afternoon, and something clicked. She'd always been beautiful. Maybe it was the way the light hit her face or glinted off her hair. Whatever the case, he'd noticed.

And that was all it took for her to occupy his every thought.

There had just been something about her that had caught his attention and he couldn't let it go. Maybe her laugh—how rare it was—but when she did it was full and deep and much too adult for someone so young. Or maybe it was those glimpses of the woman she'd be that drew him. Her hair was dark and thick as a mink's pelt and her eyes were dark chocolate and slumberous. Her lips full and unpainted and her skin smooth and flawless. She was...different.

From that moment he'd been desperate to see her. Almost like a compulsion. She'd haunted him for the last fifteen years. He hadn't realized the horrors she'd lived with on a daily basis, and he'd hated himself that he hadn't been able to stop it. There had been no good-byes between them. There hadn't been time. One day the social services van had pulled up and she was gone, despite the fact that the MacKenzies had tried desperately to adopt her as their own.

Beckett scooted out of the booth and slapped Thomas on the shoulder. "Thanks for buying my lunch. Gotta go."

He left the diner without looking back, and the sound of his friends' laughter followed him out the door. His focus was intent as he stepped on the wooden sidewalk and stood in front of the vacant shop. He could hear the sound of a saw and someone swinging a hammer, but there was no sign of Marnie. He tried the knob, but it was locked, and disappointment rose up inside of him.

For the majority of his life he'd thought of her. And when she'd left with social services he'd felt helpless, and guilt ate at him for not stopping Harley from taking her that night. He could've prevented the whole thing, but he just hadn't been strong enough.

He hadn't known how to make contact with her or even if she'd want him to after he'd let her down like he had, but several years before, while he'd been sitting at his desk late at night going over the books for the ranch, she'd come into his mind. And for the first time he said to hell with her privacy and Googled her name.

His jaw almost hit the floor when pages of information and photographs came up. Case after case she'd helped the police solve. He remembered how accurate she'd been the night she'd seen Harley kill Mitch Jones, and all he could think was what a terrible burden she must carry.

He kept up with her as the years went on, as her photography was selected for gallery showings and pictures of her surfaced where she wore chic black dresses and held onto the arm of a man who looked at her like a prize. It was then he stopped checking on her. Seeing her with another man, in another life, hurt more than it had any right to.

Beckett rattled the knob once more and then walked back to his truck. Some days it didn't pay to go to lunch.

Chapter Six

Her return to Surrender was inevitable.

For fifteen years Marnie had seen Surrender in her visions. They were sparse at first—her mind had only been so strong after she'd watched her parents die. And for the first time in her life she'd developed the control to stop the visions as they started—slamming down a heavy metal door in her mind. Trauma did strange things to the brain.

They'd taken her away on her seventeenth birthday, so she'd only spent a year in foster care. It hadn't been so bad. Actually, it had been pretty amazing. She'd had secondhand clothes that fit her and three meals a day. And there was never the hiss of the belt as it was pulled through belt loops or the sharp crack as it connected with flesh.

She'd survived. And between scholarships and working full-time, she'd managed to make her way through college. She'd taken a photography course on a whim. A way to fulfill a fine arts credit and try something new. But instead she'd found a calling. A purpose. And a way to tell stories. There was always beauty through the lens, even when life wasn't so beautiful.

After college she'd ended up in Nebraska for a couple of years, then Kentucky, Virginia, Tennessee, and Georgia. Never staying long in any one place. Never growing roots or making friends because there was an intimacy to friendship and relationships that wasn't worth the pain or heartache. She'd learned that lesson well enough. She missed Darcy terribly. And the rest of the MacKenzies as well. They'd been her true family and she hadn't even realized it. And then there was Beckett. Love like that wasn't worth it in the long run. Nothing should be so painful.

As she'd aged she'd learned to control her gift. And if she could help others like she'd needed to be helped, then she'd do whatever she could, even at the cost of being ridiculed or ostracized.

Not everyone wanted her help, but there were enough who'd witnessed her gifts with their own eyes to use her. There were some progressive police departments who wanted to solve crimes badly enough that they'd bring her in, often as a last resort. She didn't do it for money. In fact, she always refused payment of any kind. She wasn't a charlatan. And she didn't need or want the money. Growing up poor had its advantages. She was used to a frugal life of hard work.

Her time behind the camera paid the bills—taking portraits of children and shooting wedding after wedding. But it was the photographs she took outside of those events that held her heart. She was fascinated by faces. Old, young, man, woman, child. It didn't matter. Every face had a story. She'd often wondered what story hers had told as a child. And if anyone had bothered to look at it through the lens of a camera.

She'd built her portfolio over the years, and little by little, some of her pieces had started to sell. She'd scrimped and saved and opened her first studio in Savannah. And then Clive Wallace had walked through her doors one rainy afternoon and looked at her and her work with a critical eye that had immediately set her on edge. She didn't know him or even recognize his name. But he was one of the biggest art dealers in the world. And he wanted her work. And as she'd discovered later, he'd wanted her too.

Her life had been a whirlwind for almost two years—working almost nonstop and collecting enough pieces for a show in his New York gallery. It was some of the best work she'd ever done. Her focus was sharp and she thought maybe that was the life she was supposed to lead. A rags-to-riches story where good triumphed over evil.

The show was a success and the money started rolling in. And Clive became her lover, even though he was almost twenty years older and much more experienced. He was exciting and showed her things naïve girls from Nowhere, Montana, didn't often get to see. And sometimes—he was able to make her forget where she came from.

And then she'd gotten a phone call from Lieutenant Navarro in Miami. He'd seen reports about the work she'd done for other departments and he wanted her help. Off the books because his captain wasn't as open to the woowoo kind of stuff as he was.

She wasn't a stranger to the news—her face had appeared on camera several times after helping with particular cases—but she didn't crave the attention. Clive wanted her to take the job because the publicity would be good for her next showing. So they'd gotten on the next available flight and headed to Miami.

There'd been a series of kidnappings—all infants between the ages of six weeks and nine months old. The cops had tracked down a nurse at one of the hospitals and she'd admitted to selling patient information to an unknown third party. She entered the information on a website that was set up online and then they deposited money in her bank account. Two other nurses at other hospitals also confessed once the clues led to them.

But the nurses had no idea what had happened to the babies that had been kidnapped. Their involvement didn't reach that far, though they'd each be doing a stretch behind bars. But the cops were stumped on how to find the children or where they'd ended up. And the hope of finding them was almost none.

It was an extensive and brilliantly executed kidnapping network. They'd scam parents who thought they were going through legitimate channels to adopt a child, and then place the stolen child in with the parents who paid enough money.

When she and Clive had arrived in Miami they hadn't been greeted with open arms by the city or by the higher-ups in law enforcement. And to make matters worse, the media had been notified of her arrival and were waiting to greet them at the airport, turning the whole thing into a three-ring circus. She'd found out later Clive was the mastermind behind that fiasco.

It had only taken her a matter of hours to get to the bottom of things, and thank God she'd made friends at the FBI during various cases over the previous decade. Once she'd found out the mayor, the CEO of the hospital, a captain at the police department, and a state legislator were involved, she knew she needed to call in someone who could take over and get those children back to their rightful parents.

They'd been fortunate that all the data had been meticulously kept—which children were taken from which families and what state and family they'd been sent to. It was an undertaking that would take months to clear, but she'd been able to tell them where to look and who to look at.

And Clive had been right. The combination of her popularity as a photographer and the coverage from the press over the kidnapping case had made her show sell out in less than an hour. She hadn't liked the attention. And she hadn't liked the feel of using one gift to help make the other gift profitable. The whole thing felt dirty.

Then she'd found out *why* Clive had orchestrated the press to coincide with the Miami kidnappings. Unbeknownst to her, he'd signed legal documents in her name making him her business manager and in control of the majority of her assets. He also owned her name, and because her name represented the work she did, he owned that as well. She'd trusted him, and because she'd trusted him she hadn't used her powers to look and see what he was really like on the inside until it was too late.

She knew how men like Clive worked. She'd seen him in action during business deals. He was a man who got what he wanted, no matter the cost. And she'd never be able to beat him if she tried to take him to court to reclaim what was hers. He had too much money and too much influence.

But Marnie had always been resourceful. He never should've underestimated a girl who'd been raised learning how to stay out of Harley Whitlock's way. So she'd taken the money in her savings and hidden it in a different account with only her name on it. And she'd added to it when Clive gave her a small percentage of her sales every two weeks. She'd quietly told the landlord of her studio she wouldn't be renewing her lease and she'd packed her personal belongings and favorite photographs she'd taken for her personal pleasure and not one of Clive's galleries.

He'd told her repeatedly that he'd take care of her and she

never had to worry about money again. Then he'd kept her on a tight leash, doling out small amounts of "play money," as he called it, so she had to keep coming back for more.

It was about that time that the visions of Surrender went from the occasional and sporadic to every day. She knew it was time to return home, though she didn't know what waited for her there. Her visions were oftentimes restricted when it had to do with her own future. She'd see places or small flashes. Only enough to show her a direction. And that direction had led her back to Surrender.

Clive had never been abusive. Not like her father. But he was controlling. And he'd essentially bought her, though she'd been too naïve and dazzled at the time to realize it.

When she'd finally told him she was leaving, that she wanted out of their relationship and partnership, he'd spewed such filth and hatred at her that she wondered what she'd ever seen in him to begin with. But at least he'd let her walk out the door with her belongings and the small van she'd had for years to haul equipment for photo shoots.

He'd started calling the banks and cutting off her credit cards and access to them when she'd walked out the door. He'd underestimated her. She didn't care about money. She'd never had money before and it didn't matter. But she'd be damned if she'd escape one prison only to be held in another. So she'd walked out the door and toward freedom for a second time in her life, with a smile on her face.

Chapter Seven

After a busted radiator in Missouri and a stomach bug that kept her holed up for two days in South Dakota, she finally crested the hill that led to Surrender.

She stopped the car at the top, next to the sign that said *Welcome to Surrender*. It was familiar, yet different. They'd upgraded the old green sign to a white wooden one that had been hand painted.

The sun was a flaming orange ball directly overhead and the sky was cloudless. She'd forgotten how beautiful it was. Or maybe she hadn't appreciated the splendor of the landscape as a child.

Surrender was a perfect green jewel nestled in a valley of rolling hills. Farther out the land softened and flattened so it was miles of white fences and pastureland. A lake of crystal clear blue was on the west side of Surrender, but it was right in the middle of MacKenzie land and it was for personal use. To the east side of Surrender was a larger lake—one side of it bordered Hamilton land, but the other side was open to the public. She had a perfect view of everything from where she sat.

And for the first time since she'd had her art and her name taken from her, she felt the urge to get her camera out. The pictures she took now would be for her own enjoyment. She'd never needed fame or glory. She'd only needed an escape.

She didn't fight the urge. The camera bag sat strapped into the passenger seat, where it had been since she'd started her trek across the country. The sunlight was too bright to get the kind of shots she wanted, but she got one or two that might be good to frame for her new studio.

It had taken her two solid weeks to travel from Georgia to Montana between the car problems and her illness. But she'd used the travel time wisely. Her first phone call had been to Mary MacKenzie. Mary had been a second mother to her, and guilt still ate at her that she'd not been in contact with her or Darcy, either one. She'd picked up the phone several times to dial their number, but she'd never had the courage to go through with it. And then she ultimately decided that maybe it was best to leave the past in the past.

Marnie knew the MacKenzies had tried to adopt her after social services had taken her away. She'd overheard the social worker mention it while she was in the hospital being treated after that last beating. But social services ultimately thought she'd do better in a location outside of Surrender, so they'd placed her with a foster family in Bozeman.

Calling Mary out of the blue had been one of the hardest things she'd ever done. But after her initial surprise, Mary had talked with her as if no time had passed at all. By the time she hung up the phone, she had a house to rent and had been guaranteed the vacant shop next to the sheriff's office. Now all she had to do was apply for the permits and business license she needed to open the shop and she'd be all set.

Marnie packed away her camera and got back in the car. And then after a deep breath she put it in drive. No one noticed her as she drove through town. Main Street was busier than it had been during her childhood, and though there was no parking on the bricked road that ran between the middle of the businesses downtown, she'd watched people circling from her place on the hilltop, looking for a place to park.

She got lucky and a car pulled out of a spot just behind the florist shop. There was no time like the present, so she straightened her spine and put on the bored look she'd learned to adopt during her showings. She was an adult now, not a helpless child, and it didn't matter that people might stare or that there'd be whispers behind her back. This was Surrender. There would always be whispers about something.

But she was where she was supposed to be. She'd known it from the first vision she'd had after she left, the one where she'd watched Darcy lying on her bed crying because her best friend was never coming back. Marnie might not have been in Surrender in person, but she'd still seen. And when the visions changed from the present and they were instead placing her in them somewhere in the future, she knew she'd made the right decision to leave her life behind and start anew.

The air was brisk and bitter with cold despite the sun shining overhead, so she wrapped her blue quilted jacket around her and set off for the sheriff's office. She'd been in the south too long and her blood was thin. Moving back to a place that had real winters was going to take some adjustment and the thought made her smile just a little. Her first southern summer had been an adjustment too.

The florist was at the end of the street, so she followed the sidewalk around to the front of the building and stepped up on the wooden sidewalk that lined the front of each side of the street. She passed the bookstore, and a young mother and her toddler came out of the ice cream shop next door. The woman looked at her oddly since she didn't recognize her, but she smiled and said hello as she dodged the rocky road-covered hands of her child.

White rocking chairs, two on each side of the door, sat in front of the mercantile and two old men sat rocking and gossiping as she passed by. They both nodded and went about their conversation. She'd recognized them, but couldn't put a name to a face. But one of the men had once given her a pack of bubble gum for a treat when her mama couldn't afford to add anything else to the groceries in her cart. Mr. Murdock, she thought.

They wouldn't recognize her. She'd spent her entire life trying to be invisible. To blend in and not draw attention to herself. If she'd had a choice, she would've skipped her own gallery showings, but Clive had insisted she be there for them, dressed up and painted like a doll. But here, in her own clothes, she was something unremarkable.

The people who passed her would see a young woman with dark hair pulled back in a tail at the nape of her neck. Thick brows winged over dark eyes that were somber and too serious. She'd lost weight over the last few months she'd spent with Clive and her cheekbones were a little too sharp and her eyes a little too big for her face. Her clothes were simple—a thick cable-knit sweater in hunter green and a pair of dark brown corduroy pants. Her boots were well used and scuffed at the toes.

The little shop next to the mercantile was vacant and she stopped to stand in front of it and look through the windows. She knew it was the place her shop would be. There were two square display windows and the thick wooden door had a glass insert. The floors were the original wood and though the space was narrow, it was deep enough that she could divide it into two spaces—one a reception area and place to hang samples of her work, and in the other she could put backdrops and screens for in-house photo shoots. There was an apartment above the space that had a tenant, but Mary assured her that she was quiet and wouldn't be a bother.

She felt some of the tension go out of her shoulders. She could make this work. Now she just had to find the courage to actually speak to the people she'd known all her life. But she could do it. Those same people would be lining up for family portraits, graduation pictures, babies, and weddings. It was a business, and she was providing a service for the community.

It was only a few more steps to the front door of the sheriff's office, and she found her hand was slightly damp as she turned the knob. Mary had told her that Cooper had beat Sheriff Rafferty in the election several years back. She'd grown up with Cooper, just like she had all the MacKenzies, though he'd been several years older and didn't often hang out with them. But imagining him in the position of authority as sheriff was hard to wrap her brain around, especially knowing some of the stuff he'd done as a kid.

She'd grown up hearing Harley rail against the police. How corrupt and useless they were. How they targeted the poor and the people who needed their help the most. And then he'd told her if she ever told Sheriff Rafferty about the whippings that Rafferty would come straight to him because they were friends. And she'd get twice the punishment.

She'd never heard any gossip around town that Sheriff Rafferty had been corrupt. Mostly people called him inept and lazy. But she'd never been sure if her daddy was telling the truth about them being friends, so she'd made it her policy to steer clear of the police whenever she saw them.

The sheriff's office was pretty much what she'd expected. It smelled strongly of Pine-Sol trying to mask the smell of sweat and burned coffee. A wooden desk sat to the right of the door and a slightly plump woman with fresh highlights in her blonde hair sat behind the desk, her long nails clicking against the keyboard as she typed. Her desk was stacked with papers and file folders, and behind her was a dispatch board where she took calls if there was trouble.

There was another desk directly across from her, but this one was empty except for a couple of pictures of a man she'd never seen before and what she assumed was his wife, who was stunningly beautiful. Two jail cells lined the back wall of the room. They were stark and empty except for a cot with a mattress that had been covered in plastic and a metal toilet.

It took Marnie a few seconds to remember why she recognized the woman's face. And then it hit her and dread settled in her stomach like a lead ball. Lila Rose. The girl everyone loved to hate, but never had the guts to say so to her face because they were afraid of what she'd say about them.

There hadn't been a moment from kindergarten to her junior year that Lila hadn't made fun of her for wearing the same old clothes or only having a boiled egg to eat for lunch some days. It had always irked Lila that Marnie could come and go as she pleased at the MacKenzies. In her mind, Lila and Darcy should've been the best of friends. The two daughters of wealthy ranchers. But Darcy couldn't stand Lila and had told her so to her face in the first grade. In turn, Lila had set out to make Marnie as miserable as possible.

"Can I help you?" Lila said.

She was still pretty and it was easy for Marnie to see the Carnival Queen now that she'd recognized her. She must've married well, because the rock on her finger had to be a good two carats and the diamond tennis bracelet she wore strained against the thickness of her wrist.

Marnie didn't have to look into Lila's mind to see what she was thinking. It was all over her face. She sized Marnie up quickly and dismissed her as unimportant, though she was curious about what she was doing in Surrender. But she smiled a fake smile and welcomed her anyway.

"I'm here to see Cooper. I think he's expecting me."

"Oh, sure. He mentioned something about that, though he didn't tell me your name. You must be the new tenant over at the river house. I heard him mention the other day that it had been rented."

"That's me," Marnie said, forcing a smile. After all, Lila and her family were potential customers. "Is he in?"

"Oh, sure, but I think he's on a phone call. Let me check."

Marnie could tell she was irritated that she didn't introduce herself, but she wasn't quite ready for that yet. Lila got up and knocked lightly on the closed door behind her desk. She stuck her head in and said a few words and then closed the door again.

"He'll be right out," she said, taking her place behind the desk again. "Where are you moving here from? Do I detect a little bit of the South in your voice?"

"I'm coming from Savannah. I've actually rented the shop next door to open a photography studio."

Lila squealed and clapped her hands together, and Marnie wondered how it was some people never changed. She was still the same vapid popular girl, trapped inside a thirty-two-year-old body. And she'd still be that same girl at eighty.

"Oh, that's perfect! We have to drive all the way to Myrna Springs to get family photos done, and that's almost an hour away. A good friend of mine had her wedding here and she brought in a fancy photographer all the way from Billings." Lila lowered her voice a little and said, "It was the sheriff's cousin that did that, but they can afford it. Darcy always did have high and mighty taste. Must've cost a fortune."

Marnie raised her eyebrows at that and wondered how long it took Lila to spread police business all over town. She probably had her phone to her ear the minute a 911 call came in to the switchboard.

"I've done weddings big and small all over the country. Now people will be coming to Surrender to get their portraits done."

Lila's lips pinched and her eyes widened in disbelief, but she continued to smile. "You must be a good photographer if you think people will come all the way to Surrender for photos. The only time we get visitors is when it's fishing and hunting season. And those people aren't too interested in fancy photography, if you know what I mean."

Marnie kept her smile in place. "I guess I'll have to wait and see. I had a six-month waiting list when I was in Savannah."

Thankfully, Cooper's office door opened and he stepped out. Her first thought was that he hadn't changed much. The MacKenzies had all been blessed with good looks, but only a few of them possessed the black hair and blue eyes that had been passed down from their great-grandfather. Cooper, Darcy, Shane, and their nephew Jayden all shared those attributes. When it came to those four, it wasn't just good looks. They were stunning.

Her last impression of Cooper was of a young man in his twenties who'd finished his term in the military and was trying to figure out what he should do with his life. He looked rougher around the edges than he had at twenty-five. She could see the sleeve of tattoos peeking out beneath his rolled-up shirt sleeves and a growth of stubble she had to imagine was on purpose instead of him forgetting to shave.

He was tall, like all the MacKenzies were, but Cooper was just a little taller than the others. He was broad through the shoulders and chest, like a body builder, and he wore the weapon in his holster like he'd been born to it. She'd known from the start that he was destined to protect and serve. She glanced at the gold wedding band he wore and could see the contentment on his face. He'd made a good life.

"Marnie," he said, breaking out into a grin. "It's so good to see you."

He didn't try to hug her. She'd never liked being touched much, but she went up to him to shake his hand. As their skin touched, she opened herself briefly. Her smile grew wider. He was very content in his life, he loved his wife and children more than anything, and Lila annoyed the hell out of him, but he'd given her the job as a favor to her husband, whom he did like.

"It's good to be back," she said.

"Is it?" His expression sobered and he took a good look at her, watching her as a cop would instead of a friend. But only because he was genuinely concerned about her.

"I think it is," she answered. "I wasn't so sure when I decided to come home. But it feels right now that I'm here."

"Oh my goodness," Lila said, her mouth forming a little "O" before she covered it with her hand. "*Marnie Whitlock.* I never in my life would've known that was you. Just look at you all grown up and back in Surrender. It's me," she said. "Lila Rose. Well, I'm Lila Randolph now. I married Tucker Randolph. You remember him? He graduated with Cooper."

She didn't remember Tucker Randolph, but that wasn't surprising since Cooper was almost a decade older than she was. They hadn't exactly run in the same circles. She did recognize the Randolph name, though. Mr. Randolph, had to be Tucker's daddy, was the bank president.

The look on her face must've been confused because Lila pouted and put her hands on her generous hips. "Now don't tell me you don't remember me. We were in school together all the way through until you...left." She let the word hang there and her eyes glittered with malice even though her smile remained in place. "Oh, I'm sorry, honey. I didn't mean to make you remember. That must've been so hard on you when your parents died like that. And with him wanted for murder and everything." She clucked her tongue and looked like she was about to go on when Cooper interrupted.

"Lila, why don't you take your lunch break? I'll cover the switchboards until Deputy Greyson gets back. He'll only be a few more minutes."

Lila looked like she wanted to argue, but the look on Cooper's face must've changed her mind. "Sure thing, Sheriff. You want me to bring you anything back?"

"No, I'm going to meet my wife for lunch once Greyson gets back. Thanks for the offer though."

Lila grabbed her handbag out of the bottom drawer of the desk, eagerness to spread the news that Marnie was back in town practically bursting from her already tight seams. "Now, don't be a stranger, Marnie. I'd love to sit down and catch up one afternoon. And I just can't wait until your little studio opens. It's been too long since we had a family portrait taken. Not since our littlest was born. He's the cutest thing. You'll just love him."

Lila shot out the door as fast as her four-inch Louboutins would allow her, and the pregnant silence in her wake was almost like a breath of fresh air.

"I should apologize for her," Cooper said. "But it wouldn't do any good. She is who she is, and that'll never change."

"She's never bothered me. She helped thicken my skin when I was still in grade school."

"I bet," he said, shaking his head. "Tucker is a close friend of mine. Took over for his daddy as the bank president when old Mr. Randolph passed on. And he does a good job of it too. But Lila's spending habits don't fit in with a banker's salary, even as good as it is, so he told her flat out if she wanted to buy shoes that cost more than a mortgage then she could work for them herself.

"The problem was she'd never had a job before. Their youngest is three and a holy terror. The other two are in school. But she had trouble finding work without any qualifications. And my secretary was set to retire. We all do double and triple duty here, so that means she covers the switchboard for emergency calls too. It's been a real interesting adventure so far."

Marnie felt a laugh bubble from inside and it sounded foreign to her ears. When was the last time she'd laughed? In fact, when was the last time she'd done anything but work?

He grinned and said, "Come on back here to my office. I'm sure you want to get settled. Aunt Mary told you the house is furnished?"

"Yes, it's just what I needed. The timing worked out perfectly."

"It has a way of doing that." He moved behind his desk and took papers out of a file folder and then slid them across to her. "You'll need to get sheets and towels for the house, but there are dishes in the cabinet. This is the lease agreement for the house and the shop next door. Aunt Mary and Uncle Jim own both of them so the paperwork is simple enough. Everything is as y'all discussed over the phone, but I'm sure you want to look it over. I've got the keys to both places, so once you sign we're good to go."

She looked around his office. It was small and sparsely furnished. A large L-shaped desk with two computer monitors dominated the space. A file cabinet sat in the corner, and a single bookshelf that was filled with a mish-mash of books, photographs and knickknacks sat next to it.

The photographs caught her attention as they always did. The faces staring back fascinated her. A pretty woman with dark hair cut like a pixie and laughing brown eyes smiled into the camera. The look on her face was flirtatious and a little bit naughty, and Marnie knew automatically that Cooper had been behind the camera. She held two little boys on her lap, about one and three years old.

"They're beautiful," she said, touching the edge of the frame.

"I think so," he said with a smile. "But the youngest one is a handful. Aunt Mary says I'm getting what I deserve with that one."

"I'm glad you're happy. It shows."

"And I'm sorry you're not. We've always considered you as part of the family, even the years between when we didn't see you. I hope you know that."

"Oh, I do," she said, looking over the rental papers blindly so he wouldn't see the tears that filled her eyes. "This is a good start to my happiness. It's where I need to be."

"Good. Aunt Mary said to tell you to come to dinner tonight. Most of the family is going to be there. And she said no excuses because she knows you won't feel like grocery shopping and there's no food in the rental house."

"I'd never argue with Mary."

"I always said you were a smart girl."

Chapter Eight

Marnie managed to make it a full week without having to interact with anyone but the MacKenzies.

Like an obedient daughter, she'd driven to see them that first night. She'd gone early, so the late rays of the sun painted the landscape in an orange glow. She'd taken the left fork in the road by the giant oak tree like always, purposefully blocking the image of her as a girl lying beaten at its roots.

Her hands grasped tight around the steering wheel and she let out a relieved breath as distance grew between her and the fork in the road. Her van struggled to make the incline and she pressed down a little harder on the gas, coaxing it along. She didn't have the time or the money for it to stop working on her.

The van let out an audible sigh of relief when the land flattened out and she smiled as the sight of the lake and the house she'd spent so much time in as a child came into view. There were two main houses, one on each side of the lake, and James and John MacKenzie had raised their families in their respective homes until John and his wife were tragically killed, leaving four half-grown boys behind.

The houses looked the same, but different. Her attention was drawn to James and Mary's house—the house that had been her real home. They'd added on to it, a patchwork quilt of stone and rough wood that blended in perfectly with the area. Trees had grown more mature and a tire swing had been added to a sturdy branch.

But that wasn't the only thing that had changed. The barns and house that had belonged to John MacKenzie before his death—and from what she now understood belonged to Thomas—all all remained. But there was a massive concrete wall that encompassed a huge portion of the land, and there was no way to get to the house that she'd once pretended was her own without going through the gates.

Mary had called it a compound and she was right. It was intimidating and impenetrable, and Marnie felt herself start to sweat as she drove up to the big gates and the two men who stood there protecting them, even though she hadn't done anything wrong.

The two men were armed and didn't look like they possessed an ounce of good humor as they checked her ID and scanned her license plate. Then they took her fingerprints before finally signaling to someone on the other side that the gates could be opened.

Marnie had heard of MacKenzie Security of course, and she knew that it was Declan's organization and that most of the family played a part in some way. It was something they all profited from, but it came at a cost. They lived at an elevated level of danger that Marnie hadn't realized until she'd seen the security. Mary had told her they no longer took any chances after what happened to Shane. Family was too important not to protect at all costs.

Once inside the gates it didn't feel like a prison. She was sure the MacKenzies had designed it that way. There were lots of trees and the entry road speared off in three different directions. She took the one to the left and followed it down to the lake where the trees became sparser and the land opened up so it was nothing but rolling green grass and the shimmer of the lake as the sun reflected off its surface.

She'd noticed the scattering of newer homes and she assumed they belonged to various MacKenzie children and their spouses. They were spread out far enough for privacy, but they were still close enough for everyone to gather quickly if there was an emergency.

Mary and James greeted her at the door with big bear hugs, and soon after, she was enveloped in hugs from everyone, even those she'd never met. She told herself to breathe and let them hug her. That they needed the contact, even though touching them and the emotions they were feeling almost brought her to her knees.

The MacKenzie house was pure chaos and she loved it. Almost everyone was there, except for Cade and his wife Bailey, who ran the Fort Worth office of MacKenzie Security, and Darcy and her husband Brant, who ran the DC office.

"Why'd you send Darcy so far away from home?" she asked Declan.

"The farther away that little hellcat is, the more peace we all have," he said, grinning. "Besides, she's adapted well to the city. Something about being close to Nordstrom and shoes that weren't meant for trekking through manure. They'll be home for Christmas. They spend Thanksgiving down with Brant's family in Texas. Brant and Cade's wife are brother and sister, so they do their own thing."

"I don't know how you keep up with everyone. It feels like there's a thousand people in this house and they all have the last name MacKenzie."

"It feels that way to us too. Mom knocked a couple of walls out between the connecting bedrooms and made a big playroom. She had an artist come in and paint a big family tree on the wall. It's very cool because some of the branches come out from the wall and ceiling and have leaves on them. She said it was for aesthetic purposes and for the kids to enjoy, but we tease her about just needing one space where she can see everyone's names and who belongs to whom."

Marnie laughed and relaxed a little, spontaneously patting Declan on the arm in sympathy. It must have been because her emotions were raw and her walls were down, but the touch opened her to his most inner thoughts. She hadn't meant to intrude but sometimes when she was tired or upset she didn't have as much control over her power as she normally did.

"It must be nice," she said. "Having family like that."

"You have family like that too, kiddo," he said, winking. "And every time we turn around someone's getting married or a baby is being born. MacKenzie Security has offices in DC and Texas, and some of the agents that work for me are as close as brothers." He shook his head, looking perplexed. "Then there are their wives and children. It's a zoo."

"You love it," she said.

"Yeah, marriage has softened me a bit, I think."

"Not softened you. Made you more compassionate. There's a difference."

"Don't let the word get out on that. It's best if competitors and employees alike still think I'm a badass."

She laughed. "Oh, there's no question about that."

"Good. We've started branching out quite a bit. Loaning our talents out for specific jobs. Very specific jobs. I'm choosy about who we associate with."

"That seems wise."

"You can always spot anyone who's working for me around town," he said. "Newcomers stick out like a sore thumb. It doesn't matter how good at blending in they are."

"Yes, I think I met one of yours in Annabeth's shop the other day. She was very British."

Declan smiled. "Ahh, Lady Olivia. You'll like her. We're working with her and Atticus on something very time sensitive at the moment."

The scar along Declan's jaw was new since she'd last seen him, but it was the scars on the inside that made her catch her breath. Declan had lived the life of a hero—seen and done things that no man should ever have to endure—and he deserved privacy in those thoughts. The good news was his wife and children helped balance him now, and many of those scars had healed because of them.

"You'll get there in time," she assured him. "You've made a good life, Dec. I'm glad for you." She removed her hand and resisted the need to wipe it on her slacks. Seeing into Declan's mind wasn't easy. She couldn't imagine living with it.

"And you came back to Surrender to build one for yourself," he countered. "Everyone's timing is different. This is your time. Enjoy it and be patient. Don't let anyone rush you. Not even us. We can be bulldozers."

His phone rang and he pulled it from his pocket, looking at the caller ID. "Speaking of work, I've got to take this. MacKenzie Security is helping out a friend with a job."

She saw a quick flash of men—honorable men—in black BDUs and face paint, scaling walls and saving lives. "Delta Force," she said, surprising him. And then she said, "I apologize. It was just a flash."

"It's okay. They're the good guys. And we always try to help the good guys. There aren't many of them left in the world."

"You can trust Luke Brenner," she said.

"I know. But it's good to hear you confirm it." He nodded his thanks and then went into the other room to take the call.

"If you people want to eat then I suggest you get to the table and find a seat," Mary MacKenzie said, her voice carrying. "Kids' plates are already fixed and at the little tables, and no, Flynn, before you ask, you're not big enough to sit at the grown-up table yet."

"Flynn is mine," Declan said. "He's four going on forty. He thinks sitting at the kid table with his cousins is beneath him."

Someone directed her to a chair—Cat, if she remembered right from the introductions—who was Thomas's wife. It was a huge and rowdy group, a million conversations going on at the same time, and she had a hard time keeping up with any of them. It had been too long since she'd been a part of something like this, and it was all a little bit overwhelming.

It hadn't gone past her notice that Shane hadn't come to dinner, and it hadn't gone past anyone else's notice either. He was on most everyone's minds and she was getting slammed with a variety of emotions where the youngest MacKenzie son was concerned. Worry, guilt, frustration, anger, disappointment, sadness, fear, and despair. Despite the smiles on their faces and the laughter, the underlying emotions all but slapped her in the face until she thought she'd weep with the sorrow of it all.

The weight of those emotions pressed down on her and she pushed her food around on her plate, unable to eat. The thing that worried her the most was that she couldn't see Shane in anyone's future. There was just darkness there. Her visions could change depending on choices people made in life, but for now they had every reason to be concerned for Shane's well-being.

It was when she was about to leave that she heard Beckett's name brought up. The MacKenzies all shared equal responsibility for the MacKenzie Ranch, but at Big Sky Ranch there was only Beckett to oversee everything. He had a foreman and ranch hands of course, but Beckett wasn't one to not be involved in some way.

There was talk of trying to get him loose from his cows and get together like old times, and Marnie would've been lying if she hadn't purposefully slowed pulling on her coat and hat to listen to the conversation.

Beckett had occupied her thoughts since she was sixteen years old, and seeing a glimpse of him the other day as he stood in the middle of the street, embarrassed and angry, was enough to bring the dreams back her subconscious had been too embarrassed to have when she was a girl.

Even though Clive had been her lover, he'd never made her feel like what she'd felt like during the vision she'd had of her and Beckett together. In fact, Clive hadn't seemed overly interested in sex with her at all. He'd wanted her talent—was envious of it and jealous—and being intimate with her only made him resent her more.

She'd watched him from the safety of her shop, but it had only taken one glance at Beckett standing in the middle of the street to have all those feelings and needs rush to the surface again. Needs she'd repressed since the vision of the two of them under the willow had fizzled to nothing.

Just that quickly she saw them again, a hot, erotic encounter that was nothing like the first vision. It was fast and hard—sweaty bodies and tangled limbs desperate for more of each other. And just as quickly as it appeared it was gone, and she was standing shaken and breathless in the empty shop.

Her pulse had raced and her body throbbed with unquenched desire, and it was everything she could do to stumble to the little bathroom off to the side and close the door behind her. Her body was hot to the touch and all she needed was a little relief. It had been so long since she'd felt that kind of pleasure. Never with Clive. And only in her mind with Beckett. A sad and sorry existence to be sure.

She hadn't cared that it was the middle of the day and that workers might come back from their lunch break at any moment. She'd only thought about the pleasure—and that at some point in time she'd finally get to feel him against her for real.

It had only taken seconds—a quick slip of the hand beneath the lace of her panties—and her fingers thrummed quickly against her clit, bringing her to a fast, hard orgasm. She bit her lip to keep from crying out and leaned against the door so her knees wouldn't buckle.

And then she'd heard the rattle of the doorknob and the afterglow of release turned to panic at being caught. She straightened her clothes and washed her hands, and then looked at herself in the mirror. She saw flushed cheeks and eyes that held a slumberous, dreamy quality to them, and her breath came in shallow pants.

She hadn't done anything wrong. It was a completely normal reaction and she had a right to pleasure. A right to a fulfilled life. She'd had years of therapy just to be able to say that to herself.

By the time she'd gotten herself under control, whoever had been at the door was long gone.

Brought out of her reverie, Marnie hurried and put her coat on, feeling the same rush of instant arousal as the MacKenzies spoke about Beckett, and she hugged everyone quickly as she made her exit. Her dreams had gotten a lot more exciting of late, and she couldn't wait to get back to them.

Chapter Nine

Construction workers hammered away in the back room, and Marnie's head pounded along with every stroke of the hammer. For days she'd listened to the same tune—the whine of the saw and the constant whir of drills. But there was progress. At least she assumed it was progress. She supposed it was one of those instances where things had to look worse before they could look better.

The wood floor was covered with drop cloths, and ladders and tools and sawhorses were spread throughout. They'd built a wall between the reception area and the studio space, and they were putting up two more walls in the far back corner where her small office would be. The original wood floors would be refinished once everything was painted.

She'd need to hire a part-time receptionist—that was already on her long list of things to do before opening day. But the most pressing job was putting together the big desk that would be a permanent piece of furniture in the reception area. *If* she ever managed to get it put together. She was starting to regret telling the deliveryman that she could do it herself. But she'd wanted to have a hand in the building of her studio and this was her way of doing it. The only problem was it didn't look like all the instructions had been included in the box and some of the parts seemed to be missing.

"Shit," she mumbled under her breath and then looked up guiltily when someone knocked on the door.

Grant MacKenzie was James and Mary MacKenzie's second

oldest child, a couple of years younger than Cade and a couple years older than Declan. He also owned MacKenzie Construction and was in charge of all the chaos going on in her studio.

She left the pieces of desk and tools on the floor, wiped her dusty palms on her jeans, and went to answer the door. She stepped back to let him inside and the cool breeze from outside felt good against her gritty skin, the fresh air a relief from dust she'd been breathing all morning.

"Hey, Marnie. Just came to check on the progress and make sure everything is on schedule." He looked around with a carpenter's eye and nodded his head. "It's really starting to shape up."

Grant was quieter than his siblings. He was a soft spoken and a patient man, but there was no question that he was the boss. He had the height of the MacKenzies, but his hair was dark blond and his eyes a soft brown.

"I think it's going well," she answered. "I'll probably be done putting this desk together by the time we're ready to open." She winced and then said, "Maybe."

He grimaced and looked at the mess she'd made of things on the floor. "I've put that particular desk together before a couple of times. Looks like half the instructions are missing and some of the hardware. I'm supposed to meet Annabeth for lunch, but she's stuck with customers for the moment, so I'm at loose ends."

Annabeth was his wife and she owned the little clothing boutique almost directly across from her studio. She sold some beautiful things, but she was out of Marnie's price range at the moment. And photographers didn't exactly wear their best clothes to work when they spent most of their day crawling around unusual places to get the best shots.

"Why don't we make a trade?" he said. "I'll put together this desk for you and you can hang your sign."

He held up the hand-carved wooden sign that said *Captured Moments* etched on each side.

"Oh, it's finished," she said, genuinely surprised. Excitement thrummed inside of her. It was starting to be real. She was back and she was opening a business for herself. "It's beautiful. Just how I envisioned it. Thank you so much." She reached out to take it from him and gently traced the letters. "You've got a deal. That beast of a desk is all yours."

Her smile was relaxed and easy, and she realized despite her fears of coming back to Surrender that she was home. Good or bad. This was what home felt like. What she'd been missing all the years in between.

She grabbed the ladder she'd propped against the wall and took it outside while Grant rolled up his sleeves and got to work on the desk. She would've felt him coming if she hadn't been mentally cursing the little hook that refused to cooperate as she tried to hang the sign.

"Need some help?" a familiar voice said from below.

She let go of the sign to catch her balance and teetered back and forth, bumping her head on the sign as it dangled down from one hook and swayed back and forth.

"Easy there," Beckett said, his voice soothing and calm. "I didn't mean to startle you."

"It's okay. I wasn't paying attention." She looked down at his hands steadying the ladder and then took a deep breath before finally looking him in the eye. She couldn't hold his gaze for long—there was too much between them—but she did it and then focused on climbing down the ladder so she could be on solid ground.

He looked good, was all she could think as her brain struggled to catch up to reality. He'd grown from the lanky and fit teenager she remembered to a man who looked like he'd gotten his muscles from hard work instead of the inside of a gym. A soft blue shirt stretched across broad shoulders and he wore a darker blue flannel over it like a jacket. His jeans were worn and his boots had seen better days.

His hair was gilded at the tips and the waves were unruly and a little bit long. His face was bronzed from the sun and lines fanned out from the corners of his eyes when he smiled. There was a sickle-shaped white scar at his chin that hadn't been there when she'd known him before.

"I'd heard you were back in town," he said.

She rolled her eyes before she could help herself. "You and everyone else. Lila Rose spread the news faster than wildfire."

He smiled and said, "My daddy always used to say find what

you're good at and stick with it. At least she's consistent. News like that is what keeps this town going."

"I know," she said. "I haven't been gone that long. And I witnessed your little showdown the other day with Hazel. I guess I should probably thank you for taking some of the attention away from me."

He winced and she could feel the turmoil inside him. Beckett had never liked for anyone to hurt or be hurt, even if they deserved it, and she immediately regretted bringing it up.

"She's lying, you know," she said instead.

"I know. But it makes me feel better to hear you confirm it. She's got too much pride and doesn't like to lose, and she's vindictive on top of it. It's not a good combination. But my reputation will weather the storm. She's going to have to live with that little stunt the rest of her life."

Marnie almost asked him what he'd seen in Hazel in the first place, but she took a step back and told herself it wasn't any of her business what he did in his personal life.

* * * *

It was different seeing her up close and in person rather than in pictures he'd found on the Internet.

The pictures didn't show that she was just a little too thin. Or that when she let down her guard, sadness and defeat crept into her eyes. He'd known her as a child and a teenager. And even though he hadn't known about the abuse or what kind of hell she'd lived in, she'd still managed to have that solid core and determination that had been part of her appeal. Now, she just looked—tired.

He'd never gotten over what had happened fifteen years before—from their first kiss to the moment he watched Harley drag her away, to the second he got the news that the truck had been found burned to a crisp at the bottom of Hollow Gorge and two bodies had been found inside. He'd literally been sick to his stomach at the thought of what she must've endured.

And now that he was looking at her again, face to face, he wanted to hold her close and make the sadness disappear. He wanted her trust and a second chance at what they'd started so long ago. He wouldn't push her, though. She looked like a trapped animal, her eyes wide and her stance leaning back, looking for a way to escape if she needed one. The first order of business was to get her to trust him again.

"Are you going to let me help you with your sign or are you going to be stubborn about it?"

"I can do it," she said, her back stiffening.

"I know you can do it. But sometimes it's nice to take help when it's offered. It's called being neighborly."

She stared at him a few seconds and then stepped out of the way. "I wouldn't want to be accused of being unneighborly."

"Can't say I blame you," he said, climbing onto the ladder and bending the hook just a little so it fit the sign better. "You think Lila is talking about you now, just wait until she hears about that."

Beckett got the sign attached and then climbed back down the ladder. They both stared at it instead of each other, and the significance of what that sign meant weighed heavy on him. That sign meant permanence. She was back and she was back to stay. He could be patient. However long it took.

"I'll tell you what," he said. "Because I don't want people around here to get the wrong impression about you being unneighborly, I've got an idea I want to run by you."

"I can't wait to hear it," she said deadpan, an eyebrow arching and a sparkle in her eyes that hadn't been there a moment ago.

"Do you cook?"

She paused a second before answering. "I've been known to."

"What about baking? Do you make pies? Cakes? Brownies?"

"I can't imagine what you're getting at, Hamilton, but I think you're up to funny business."

He held his hands up in an innocent gesture. "I've only got your best interests at heart. I was just going to say that if you want to practice being neighborly maybe you could rustle up something sweet to eat and bring it by the house later on. I figure you might need some practice before really getting into the thick of things."

She tried to look stern, but a smile formed on her lips. "I don't think so," she said.

"Sure, I've got it. You're busy tonight. How about tomorrow night?"

"Listen...Beckett..."

"That doesn't sound good. You know I'm just going to keep asking. It's been fifteen years, Marnie. We were friends once."

"I don't have the time or energy to pick up where we left off right now. All I can be is friends."

"Ah, ha!" he said. "You said right now. Which means if I keep asking you'll eventually say yes."

She rolled her eyes. "I've learned some hard lessons in my life. And the most important is that I'm better off on my own. Someone like me..." She shrugged and the empty gesture broke his heart. "Let's just say people are usually better off staying away from me. I can't help what I am."

"That's the thing, Marnie. I've always liked you for who you are. That'll never change. And if you bothered to look you'd see that you can trust me."

"I don't want to look," she countered. "How could you ever trust me if you know I could just slip inside whenever I wanted and see your thoughts?"

"I'd say it'd save me a hell of a lot of time in trying to explain things. Believe me, if I had my way I'd love to be able to read a few thoughts now and then. Women confuse the hell out of me, and it'd be nice to know what you were thinking at least some of the time. But your head has always been hard as a rock, so I probably couldn't penetrate it anyway."

"Insulting me doesn't sound like the neighborly thing to do."

"That was a compliment, sweetheart. Why would I want to get involved with a woman with a soft head? That makes no sense."

"You're ridiculous."

"And charming as ever. If you can't make a good chocolate cake I'm also partial to brownies."

She had to laugh. "No."

"Good thing I've always been patient."

She folded up the ladder and moved toward the door of her shop. "I've got a lot of work to do," she said, trying to dismiss him. "And I'm sure you need to go play with your cows."

Beckett grinned at the not-so-subtle attempt to get rid of him. Yeah, she had some spine left in her after all. Damned if that didn't turn him on.

"Why don't you read my mind now, Marnie?" he said, arching a brow in challenge.

Her lips twitched. "I don't have to. You're not very subtle."

"It's good to see you again," he said, serious this time. He reached out his hand to shake hers, to dare her to touch him. And when she did the heat from her hand sizzled up his arm like an electric current. Their gazes locked and they stood frozen, waiting to see who would let go first.

"You'd better leave," she said, letting go of his hand and taking a step back. "Your mother is trying to reach you. You should probably answer her phone call."

Beckett sighed. "I don't suppose you want to tell me what she's going to say so I can have a good answer ready."

"Nope, you're on your own on this one. My advice would be to just stay quiet and listen. And when she calls you a bonehead remember she's doing it out of love."

"Right. That's one of her favorites. Thanks for the warning, though I'd have preferred the brownies."

"Good-bye, Beckett," she said, but there was a smile on her face now and he felt lighter of heart.

He saluted and headed toward the sheriff's office to where he'd parked his truck. But he turned around before she could go inside.

"Oh, and Marnie," he said, "I'm going to keep asking. I just wanted to warn you first."

"As long as you don't mind that I'll keep saying no."

"I don't mind at all." He winked and walked away, deciding there were some women put on earth that were meant to make men do foolish things.

Chapter Ten

Instead of heading back to his truck and toward home where work was waiting for him, Beckett decided there was no time like the present for foolishness. He veered from his truck back across the street toward the bakery. The pleasure of stepping inside and inhaling fresh baked bread and pastries was short lived when he saw Denny Trout in line.

Denny was Hazel's older brother and he was the foreman for the Caldwell's over at the Circle C Ranch. Circle C had fallen on rough times the last decade or so, and a lot of people said that it was because of Denny. He spent more time gambling than he did doing his job. People also said the reason he hadn't been let go was because he spent more time doing Isobel Caldwell than he did gambling. There were at least fifteen years between Denny and Isobel, but the affair had been going on since before Denny had become foreman.

Isobel's husband, George, didn't seem to mind the affair as he much preferred to warm their housekeeper's bed instead of his own wife's. Granted, the Caldwell housekeeper was something to look at, though George didn't let her get out much. George was a jealous sort and he'd once bashed in Jed Blanchard's windshield with a tire iron for wolf whistling at her while she was shopping at the mercantile.

Beckett would've put money down that the girl wasn't legal drinking age, and if she was she wasn't far past it. George was somewhere in his mid-fifties, but Beckett's mama had always said

George had a taste for the young ones.

Maybe if both the Caldwells had been more interested in breeding and selling their cattle at top dollar instead of jumping in and out of other people's beds, they wouldn't be selling off a chunk of land to pay off all their debts. As it was, Beckett had already made arrangements to purchase the land at a fair price since it bordered the far side of his property.

"Well, look who it is," Denny said loud enough to get everyone's attention. The noise from those sitting and enjoying afternoon cups of coffee and sweets died down to nothing.

"Denny," Beckett acknowledged and then got in the back of the line. The smart thing to do would've been to turn around and leave. But his male pride wasn't going to back down from a worthless son of a bitch like Denny.

Denny turned in a slow circle to make sure he had a captive audience. He had a shit-eating grin on his face and Beckett knew this wasn't going to end well.

"Better watch out, ladies," Denny called out. "Lover boy here likes to stick that famous prick into whatever walks by and leave you high and dry when he plants a bastard in you. Better cross your legs."

There were a few snickers, but Beckett stayed silent and kept his gaze straight ahead.

"Saw you walk over from the new place next to the sheriff's office," Denny said. "By the way you were hanging all over that woman, I say you've moved on pretty quickly from my sister."

"Your sister and I were never something I had to move on from. It was what it was. Nothing more."

"You calling my sister a liar?" Denny said, stepping out of line. "She said you promised her all kinds of things. Marriage and that big fancy house you live in. High and mighty Hamilton's on the hill."

"If she told you all that then yes, I'm calling her a liar."

Denny charged at him and Beckett was braced for it, but a sharp voice from behind the counter stopped him in his tracks.

"Denny Trout, don't you lay one finger on him in my shop," Mrs. Baker said. "Do you understand me? I'll call the sheriff right now if I have to."

Denny froze, his mouth in a snarl and his breath heaving in and out. He resembled a charging bull. He stared Beckett down for a few seconds and then got back in line and placed his order without saying another word. And then he started talking again, though this time he kept his gaze straight ahead while Mrs. Baker put his order together.

"I thought I recognized the woman you were talking to. She sure filled out since last time I saw her in high school. She used to creep me out with those big eyes and the spooky way she used to know things. People say she's cursed. I say she's one of those phonies on the TV looking for a quick buck."

Beckett didn't answer, but Denny sure had everyone's attention. Anyone who cared to would know about Marnie's psychic abilities. It didn't matter if what Denny said was false—he was giving them more gossip to chew on and expand to their liking.

"She hasn't been here but a couple of weeks," Denny continued. "I bet she's already spreading those long legs for you. Word has it that her daddy got her all nice and used up first so she could get out in the world and earn her keep. How much you paying her? I didn't realize y'all let trash into Hamilton House."

A red haze of anger flushed through Beckett's body, and his hands fisted down at his side. Denny chuckled and paid for his things, grabbed the bakery bag, and then walked by Beckett with a smug smile.

"Let me know when you decide to throw away the trash. I've always heard girls like that are a good ride."

Beckett's hand reached up and grabbed Denny by the collar, and he lifted him clear off the ground, even though Denny had him in height by a couple inches.

"You're going to want to steer clear of me, Denny. And you're especially going to want to steer clear of Marnie. She'd tear you up and spit you out. I'm going to tell you this one time, and let that be your warning. I won't fight you over Hazel. She's not worth it, and despite the lies she's told she was never anything more than a few rolls in the hay. And that's been months ago at that. She's lying about being pregnant and it's your family who'll have to deal with the shame of those lies.

"But Marnie is someone I'll fight for. I'd better never hear another word about her ever come out of your mouth. I don't want to hear that you started rumors about her father, her, or anyone else. Because I can promise you that Isobel Caldwell is going to get pretty bored with you without those balls you're so proud of."

Denny's face was turning red, a combination of lack of oxygen and anger, and his hands were gripped around Beckett's wrist. Mrs. Baker was quiet behind the counter, her eyes wide, and every other eye on the place was on them.

"Get out of my face," Beckett said, and dropped him to the ground. "I've already wasted enough time on you today."

Denny straightened his shirt and glared at Beckett on his way out the door. "Better watch your back, Hamilton. This is far from over." He slammed the door behind him, the little bell ringing wildly, and the entire room seemed to collectively breathe again.

Chapter Eleven

Cooper MacKenzie was a patient man.

He had to be in his line of work. He'd been a cop for a lot of years and dealt with a multitude of situations—ranging from the absurd to unspeakable tragedies. But he could say for certain he'd never been in a position quite like the one he was in now.

He and his wife, Claire, had gotten into the habit of eating their lunch together each day, a simple enough task since she worked just down the street at the library. They'd grab something at the diner and then head back to their jobs for the rest of the day. It was a comfortable routine and one he enjoyed.

So he was surprised to get a text message from Claire saying she was making lunch for them at home today and to let her know when he was on the way. His first thought was to tell her to go ahead without him. It was almost a twenty-minute drive to their house from downtown, and by the time he got there they'd hardly have any time for lunch.

He'd been texting just that when he changed his mind. She'd gone to the trouble to make lunch for both of them and he didn't want to let her down. He told Deputy Greyson he was taking some extra time for lunch but that he'd be on call if he was needed.

"No worries, Sheriff. Danny and I are both on duty and Brooks comes on for the night shift. We're covered."

"And if all else fails you've got Lila to back you up," Cooper said with a grin.

"No offense, but if we need backup I'll just call my wife."

"Probably the wiser choice."

Cooper tipped his hat and grabbed the keys to his Tahoe. By the time he took the fork in the road that led to MacKenzie land, he'd already gotten two phone calls and a dozen texts about what had happened between Denny and Beckett at the bakery.

Cooper had always been amazed at Beckett's self-control. The MacKenzies liked to fight. It had been a rite of passage in their household. Something brothers did to show their affection. And also a way for them to band together if someone tried to pick on one of them.

Beckett had been closer to Cooper's younger brothers and cousins, but he'd always had a cool head about him. Something the MacKenzies needed from time to time. If it had been anyone but Beckett, Denny Trout would've ended up in the hospital after some of the things he'd said.

Cooper looked at the clock on the dashboard and winced. Time was of the essence. He had a stack of reports to be signed on his desk and he needed to write an article for the newsletter the city sent out every month. With winter coming it was a good idea to do something on safety and supplies to carry in the car if stuck in a winter storm.

He ran through a checklist in his head and waved at the guards as they opened the gates and let him through.

He and Claire had built a home on MacKenzie land after their first year of marriage. It had a long, gravel driveway and was nestled between trees that had already lost their leaves.

It was a modest-sized white house with a wide wraparound porch. Ferns hung from hooks and rocking chairs graced both the front and back porch. The back looked out over the lake and the mountains, and he thought it'd be nice to have their lunch out there, though the temperature had dropped and it might be too cold.

His mind was occupied with thoughts of calling Beckett to see what happened and his rumbling stomach, so he was completely unprepared to open the front door of his home and see his wife standing there. In hardly anything.

His cock went rock hard in an instant. She always had that effect on him, and between work and their small children, intimacy wasn't always so easy to come by. Thank God she was a devious woman.

He and Claire had always liked to play. They'd met while he was working undercover for the DEA at a BDSM club, and they'd asked Cooper to take that particular job because it was well known that he enjoyed his sex a little…different. He fit in that world as smoothly as he did the real world. It was all part of the job, and he was one of those people who looked for the adrenaline rush wherever he was.

He'd been focused on the job and the cartel leader that had been making himself too much at home in their territory and slipping large quantities of a new drug from Colombia through the United States and into Canada. Business had been good for Rafael Morda.

And during the chaos of the wild pump of bass through the club, the gyrating half-naked bodies, and Morda positioned like a king on his throne, in walked Claire. All the available submissives in the club practically ran to get her attention, and half the Doms did too. She exuded confidence and power, and they were drawn to her like a moth to a flame. She was his equal in every way, and he'd been more surprised than anyone to find out what a small-town librarian wore beneath her clothes.

His wife had hidden secrets and he adored every one of them. He took off his gun belt at the door and laid it on the entry table. Then he tossed his cell phone beside it, thoughts of work draining out of his head with all the blood.

"This wasn't the kind of lunch I had in mind, but I'm game," he said, his eyes moving over her body slowly. "I find I'm very hungry all of a sudden."

Her black hair was sleek and short and her eyes were made up for seduction. Her lips were red and full and thoughts of them wrapped around his cock had him unsnapping the top button of his jeans for a little breathing room.

She flicked the riding crop in her hand and shook her head, telling him without words that she was in charge and to not get too aggressive. They were both dominant personalities, in and outside of the bedroom, and though Cooper had always been the Dominant in his past relationships, he couldn't get by with that with Claire.

She didn't mind submitting to him, as long as the next time they switched roles. And it looked like this was next time.

Her arms and shoulders showed muscles from her thrice weekly workouts and she wore a black corset that cinched her in the middle and pushed her very voluptuous breasts impossibly high. The bra cups of the bustier were missing so her breasts were completely bared to him, and in place of the usual gold hoops she wore at her nipples were long gold dangles.

Her skin was pale and smooth and flawless, and a tiny black triangle covered her pussy. Images of tearing the lacy scrap had him growling low in his throat. She wore leather boots that crisscrossed all the way to the middle of her thighs and she tapped the crop in her hand impatiently.

She made a hell of a picture, and the thought went through his mind that maybe it wasn't her turn to be on top after all. He wanted to throw her over his shoulder and roar with triumph as he conquered her. The Alpha in him applauded the notion, but the other side of his brain said it would be worth it if he complied with her wishes.

Twenty minutes later he wondered if she might be trying to kill him. She'd strapped him to the bed. Sneaky wench. And he had no choice but to lie there and take the torture.

She'd started at his mouth, distracting him, tempting him until he'd felt the first clasp around his wrist. And then she'd kissed her way down to his neck, taking sharp little nips with her teeth and driving him crazy. She tugged at the rings in his nipples and then her mouth replaced her fingers.

"God, Claire," he said between gritted teeth. His cock was hard enough to drive nails and his hips nudged against her. She was straddling his thighs and he almost cheered when he realized the panties she wore were crotchless and he could slide right in.

"Tsk, tsk," Claire said, shifting her hips and thwarting his chances of thrusting deep inside her. "You're always so impatient. I'm trying to have my lunch." Her smile was devious and a little bit wicked.

"You must be starving," he said. "Don't let me stop you."

"Famished," she purred.

His body was damp with sweat and he writhed on the cool

sheets as she continued her torture, her mouth tugging one last time on the nipple ring. She kissed a straight line down his taut abs and the dangles from her nipple ring trailed over the tip of his cock. His whole body shuddered at the touch and he strained against the restraints at his wrists, the headboard creaking with his strength.

He looked down his body and met her witchy gaze, and then her tongue flicked out and toyed with the silver bar at the tip of his dick and he was lost. Her mouth was a miracle, and his balls drew up tight as she swallowed him whole. He wouldn't last long at this pace and he wanted to have his lunch too.

Somewhere in the far recesses of his mind he heard his cell phone ringing from the foyer where he'd left it on the table, but he ignored it, thinking he could've been wrong and it might just be the ringing in his ears.

"Ride me," he said, his grip tightening on the restraints.

"There's time for that yet. This is going to be a long lunch."

"Not if you don't slow that sweet mouth down a little, sugar."

Her nails scraped down his thighs and she got up on all fours. "That hurts my feelings. Where's your faith in me? You don't think I could get you hard again?" She pouted prettily and leaned down so the piercings dangled against his legs, rocking back and forth in a hypnotic motion.

No, she was right. He must've lost his mind for a moment. She'd always been able to get him hard. Time after time through the night. She was insatiable. And he was insatiable when he was with her. "Jesus, Claire. I could come just by looking at you."

"Mmm, maybe next time. I've got plans for now."

She levered herself up so she stood above him on the bed and grabbed hold of the harness she'd set up before he'd gotten home. Their sex life had always been spectacular, and they liked to experiment. None of that had changed after marriage. They still had the standing toy chest and had added to it over the years. Their bed was solid and they'd had the rings installed at the corners of the headboard and footboard, as well as the hooks in the ceiling so they could attach apparatus as they wanted or needed. It seemed Claire was definitely in an experimental mood.

"I've got a surprise for you," she said.

"I'm not sure I can take any more surprises today."

She took hold of the harness in the ceiling with one hand and then hooked one thumb beneath the lacy strap of her panties and tugged. It tore and the thin scrap of lace fluttered to the bed. She stood before him, her pussy bare and the little gold ring on her clit peeking out.

"Are you sure?" she asked. She reached up with her free hand and played with the nipple ornament.

"I don't know," he said, grinning. "Give me a hint and I'll tell you whether or not I can take it."

Her grin answered his. "Oh, you'll take it. And you'll like it."

"I always do, sweetheart. Now why don't you put your money where your mouth is and share the surprise?"

"Telling you would take the fun out of it. You'll have to find it if you want it."

He arched a brow at the evasive answer and his cock jerked in anticipation. "You've got my hands tied, sugar."

He jerked against his restraints and shrugged as if there wasn't much more he could do. He knew her well. Knew when she'd reached the point where dominance took a back seat to the pleasure she sought. The less he begged, the sooner she would get down to giving him what they both wanted.

"I'll give you a hint," she said, and then she pouted prettily as the bedside phone rang.

"I'm on call," he said, voice strained.

"Well, isn't that awkward?" she said with a cheeky grin. "At least it's going to be."

And before he could stop her she used the harness to swing down to the side of the bed and hit the button for speakerphone. He didn't know how she managed to move so gracefully. It was something as simple as breathing for her.

"Coop, are you there?" Beckett asked, his voice tinny as it filled the room.

Sweat dripped from Cooper's temples and he closed his eyes, trying to get his brain cells in working order.

"I'm here." His voice was hoarse and he cleared his throat.

"Tried your cell, but Lane said you'd gone home for lunch, so thought I'd take a chance. You feeling okay? You don't sound so good."

"Think I'm coming down with a cold." Cooper shook his head in warning at Claire as her mouth quirked devilishly. He knew that look. She was up to no good. "And maybe a fever. I'm taking the rest of the day off."

Claire fluttered her eyelashes and nodded enthusiastically, and then she crawled back onto the bed, nipping at his thigh.

"I won't take up much of your time then," Beckett continued. "I just wanted to let you know what happened between me and Denny Trout down at the bakery before you hear it from anyone else."

Cooper sucked in a breath as Claire turned away from him and straddled herself over his straining erection. It was then he saw the surprise she'd alluded to earlier and he almost swallowed his tongue. Her ass was lush and round and she bent forward on her knees, showing him a perfect view of the clear disc that covered her anal passage. She was wearing a plug, and if possible his cock went even harder at the thought that he'd get to explore that passage soon.

Claire sank down on his cock, taking it inch by inch, and he tried to stifle a moan as she seated herself reverse cowgirl to the hilt. From the snug fit of her pussy, she must've been wearing one of the larger anal plugs.

"Coop, you okay? You really sound terrible."

"Never been better," he said between clinched teeth. "I've already heard about you and Denny from about twenty people." His breath hissed out as Claire looked over her shoulder and winked. And then she began to ride and any hope of keeping up with the conversation was lost.

"Just wanted to give you a heads-up. He's out for blood."

"Then watch yourself," he managed to say. "Denny's always been mean and he doesn't care if he gets caught. He's got a sheet as long as my arm of batteries and assaults. Several of them domestic with his first wife."

Cooper tested the restraints around his wrists once more and heard the headboard creak. And then he pulled harder, until the wood cracked and splintered and his hand was free.

"10-4, Coop," Beckett said. "I'm going to let you go before your fever reaches its breaking point. Make sure you tell Claire hello for me."

The phone disconnected just as Cooper managed to break his other hand free from the restraints. Claire turned her head and her red mouth gasped a perfectly round "O."

"I'll let you be the boss the next two times," he said, flipping their positions in a powerful motion so she was on all fours and he was mounted behind her. "I swear. But right now I'm going to fuck that sweet ass you teased me with."

She was soaking wet and her muscles clenched around his cock as he made the promise of what was to come.

"Mmm, I sure hope so. Otherwise I've been wearing this thing all morning for nothing."

He choked out a laugh and carefully removed the lubed plug from her anus, tossing it aside. "You wore it to work this morning?"

She held still as he lined up his cock with the stretched hole of her ass, and then as he began to penetrate she pushed back against him, taking him quickly, though not necessarily easily. He was a big man, and even with the proper preparation it took time and care. But she had other plans and began coming before his cock was buried all the way inside her.

The time for words and teasing was long gone, and only the animalistic sounds of hot, sweaty sex filled the room.

Cooper's fingers bit into her hips and then without warning an orgasm more powerful than any he'd experienced exploded from the depth of his balls. His shout filled the room and blackness clouded his vision as he held onto her like an anchor in the storm. He collapsed and barely managed to turn before he crushed her with his weight. And before they both drifted to sleep he thought his fever might last well into the weekend.

Chapter Twelve

The next morning, Marnie lay in bed, waiting for her racing pulse to slow and her body to stop vibrating from the climax she'd just had. Her dreams definitely had a mind of their own. Not that she was complaining, but it was something of a disappointment to wake up with the memory of a hard male body pressing her into the mattress only to find herself alone.

It hadn't even been twenty-four hours since their first meeting and she wanted Beckett more than she ever had. Which made her all the more resistant. Her power wouldn't dictate her future. It was a dangerous trap to fall into, and one could spend a lifetime waiting for the future to unfold, only to find out too late a certain road should've been traveled to get there, but was instead missed.

She was going to learn to live on her own. She was going to discover who she really was. And she was going to heal. Nothing would make her rush the process. Not even Beckett Hamilton. And in the meantime, she could live with the dreams. It certainly helped her start off the day relaxed.

Marnie loved the house on the river. It was exactly what she needed—seclusion and privacy and a little bit of a fairy tale.

It was a small stone cottage nestled behind a bank of trees, and it couldn't be seen from the road. In fact, she'd missed her turn into the narrow drive on more than one occasion. The stone was dark gray and black shutters flanked the windows. The sidewalk was graveled and snaked to the front porch.

The house was furnished, just as Cooper had told her, and

she'd been able to find plain white cotton sheets at the mercantile and a set of towels in the same color. Everything was simple and comfortable, just as she preferred it, and she'd turned the second bedroom into a small office.

But the master bedroom was her favorite. The walls were painted a smoky gray and trimmed in white. The bed dominated the room—the ornately carved posts thick as a tree trunk—and the bedspread was a waterfall of shades of gray that matched the walls. But the centerpiece of the room was the large picture window that looked out over the river. There was a window seat with stuffed cushions and pillows that was perfect for relaxing with a good book. She especially liked it first thing in the morning, when the fog crept over the river and through the trees like smoky fingers.

She was an early riser, but she stayed in bed, watching the show until the sun's rays shone through the window and prodded her to put her feet on the floor. The wood floors of the house were cold, so she put on the slippers and bundled up in her robe to go start the coffeemaker.

Part of Marnie wished she could avoid Beckett forever. Life had taught her some hard lessons. The most important being that the only person she could ever trust was herself. The second being that everyone had an agenda or something they wanted from you.

Her father had kept her around as a punching bag, and every once in a while he'd ask her a question like she was his own personal crystal ball. But she'd rarely been able to give him the answers he'd been seeking. Clive had wanted to possess every part of her. To own her. And he had. She'd let him because there had always been that fear that if she did the wrong thing or displeased him, he'd turn into a version of her father.

She didn't know what Beckett wanted from her yet, other than the obvious. Back before she'd left the first time, Beckett had been as young and naïve as she was. But he was a man now and she wondered what his ultimate goal was where she was concerned.

The other part of her, the less cautious part, longed to see him. The visions had led her back to Surrender, but they hadn't shown her the future. Only that she was where she belonged. She knew their paths would cross again. It was inevitable. Just as she knew they'd eventually be lovers. But it would be on her terms. She wasn't willing to give any part of herself away again. She'd already given too much, and there wasn't much left.

Her focus was going to be her business and making a life for herself at the little house on the river. Maybe once she was feeling more comfortable she'd socialize outside of the MacKenzie circle. And maybe once she'd ventured out she'd take Beckett to her bed. But for now she was content with her own company.

She stood at the kitchen window, drinking her coffee and letting her mind wander when she heard the crunch of tires coming up the drive. A white Jeep she didn't recognize skidded to a halt and she recognized the girl who'd claimed she was carrying Beckett's child when she hopped out and slammed the door.

Marnie stepped out onto the front porch so the girl wouldn't barge in. She seemed like the kind of person who would enter without an invitation. Blowing on her coffee, she took a sip and waited for the explosion that was about to come.

"You bitch!" Hazel said as she marched up the sidewalk and onto the porch steps. "How dare you think you can horn in on my man? He's mine! Do you hear me?"

Marnie stared at her several seconds, long enough to have the girl shifting from foot to foot as she waited for the argument to escalate.

"I hear you, but interestingly enough, I don't know you. Maybe you'd like to introduce yourself before you start calling me names on my own property."

"Don't act all high and mighty with me. My brother told me you were nothing but common trash. As far as my name, it's soon to be Hazel Hamilton."

"Ah, yes. I recognize the screech of your voice from your little episode in town the other day. And I guess your brother is right. I grew up about as poor as anyone could, but at least I have manners. Is that all you came to say to me? I've got to get ready for work."

Hazel's eyes narrowed at the dismissal and her face turned red, like a child throwing a tantrum. Marnie realized that's exactly what she was. A spoiled brat.

"You were all anyone could talk about last night down at

Duffey's. How your daddy beat the shit out of Beckett back when you were kids cause y'all were fucking and got caught."

"Is that what they say?" Marnie asked, brow raised in simple curiosity.

"Well, I'm here to tell you you'd better think twice about rekindling old flames. They were also saying he was sniffing around you yesterday afternoon and you were like a bitch in heat, ready to roll over right there on Main Street."

"Must be an interesting crowd you hang with. So full of information. Like I said, I've got to get ready for work, and I'm out of the mood to deal with little girl tantrums. Actually, if you'll hold on a second I'd love to get my camera. I make my living snapping interesting pictures of faces. I'd call yours *Petulance*."

Hazel shrieked like a steam whistle and her fists bunched at her side. "You bitch!"

"You're starting to repeat yourself and I'm bored. Go home to your mother and grow up."

Hazel took several steps forward and Marnie straightened to her full height. "Don't take another step. You're on my land and I won't hesitate to have you thrown behind bars for tresspassing."

"You're probably fucking the sheriff too," she spat.

"Make sure you tell him that. I'm sure it'll help lessen your time behind bars. I notice you haven't mentioned the baby. I guess that didn't pan out the way you wanted it to."

Hazel stamped her foot and fisted her hands on her hips. "I'm going to make you wish you never stepped foot back in Surrender."

"Little girl, I grew up under the fist of Harley Whitlock. If you think your tantrums scare me then you've got another thing coming. Go lick your wounds in private and stop making a fool of yourself. You spend a couple more nights down at Duffey's, I'm sure you can find a cowboy that'll make you forget all about Beckett Hamilton."

Hazel turned sharply on her heel and got back into her Jeep, slamming the door and revving the engine before she sped away.

"Yet another reason to stay away from Beckett," Marnie muttered, letting the screen door close softly behind her as she went back inside. He was nothing but trouble.

Chapter Thirteen

Marnie didn't know whether to curse Lila Rose or give her a big hug.

She'd had nonstop phone calls from people wanting to set up appointments for three solid weeks. And if they couldn't reach her by phone, they were coming by the studio and knocking on the door. Everyone wanted to get new pictures taken before the holidays, and several had asked if she could do Christmas cards.

Grant and his team were working nonstop, though they'd had a setback due to the fact that someone had thrown a brick through her front door during the middle of the night. They'd turned the deadbolt through the hole in the door and let themselves in, doing some damage to the walls and some of the framed photographs.

Downtown Surrender was virtually empty at that time of night, except for the few tenants that lived above some of the shops. And the culprit had waited until the deputy on duty had left the office next door to go on patrol. It was all very quick and the destruction to the inside seemed more of an afterthought as they'd picked up whatever tools had been left lying around to punch holes in the walls and scratch the surface of the desk.

Hazel's presence hit her in the face the moment she'd walked in to see the damage, but she hadn't acted alone. Someone else's essence had been there as well. Marnie mentioned to Cooper about the little confrontation at the house between her and Hazel, so he went out to question her, but according to Hazel's mother, she'd been out of town visiting friends during the break-in and she wouldn't be back for another week.

Most of the damage had been cosmetic and was easily fixable, but it was still a personal attack and Marnie wasn't about to let the guilty get away with it. But she could bide her time and be patient. Hazel couldn't hide forever, and Marnie had worked too hard to just roll over and take it. If she did it once Hazel would do it again and again.

She was at least able to schedule delivery for all the supplies she'd ordered while Grant and his team did the repairs. Photography wasn't for the faint of heart or wallet. Especially not if you wanted to do the job right.

Canvas, stretchers, presses, computers, printers, screens, backdrops, props—they took up a lot of room and were costly investments, but she couldn't do the job without them.

When she had a camera in her hand, something inside her changed. She wasn't the abused little girl she'd once been, and she wasn't Clive Wallace's trophy to be shown like he'd created her or cultivated her talent himself. The camera was hers and hers alone.

And as the days and weeks went by, she found herself out in the community, capturing the lives of the people she'd always observed as an outsider—smiles and tears, joy and sorrow, hope and desperation—it was life. And Surrender was teeming with it.

Beckett had stayed true to his word. He kept asking. And she kept saying no, reminding herself each time of the scene with Hazel. She couldn't let herself get involved in another relationship. She'd felt repression at the hands of her father and her lover, and she'd promised herself she'd never let anyone have that kind of control over her again. That kind of power. But Beckett was starting to wear on her.

It had started the day after their initial meeting, the same morning she'd been paid a visit from Hazel. She'd been in the back, going over paint samples with Grant, when there'd been a knock at the door. Her head had been pounding after the scene with Hazel, and she wasn't in the mood for visitors.

She knew there was going to be gossip when she returned to Surrender. She'd expected it. But she'd be lying if she said it didn't bother her that they were talking about her down at Duffey's. That Hazel's brother had called her common trash. Words hurt. No matter how thick your skin. It was how one reacted to them that mattered. But sometimes she wondered how strong she really was. What her breaking point was. Harley had never been able to break her, no matter how bad the beating. But sometimes she wished he had.

It wasn't like she'd gone to a lot of trouble to keep her gift a secret over the last decade or so. Not when she'd been helping the police in such a public manner. But it still stung to walk down the street and have people avoid her gaze or walk in the opposite direction—like she was going to chase them down and list all their sins out in public. It was almost comical. It would've been if it hadn't hurt so much.

The delivery boy on the other side of the door must've heard the gossip too, because he looked at her like she was a ghost and practically shoved the basket into her hands as soon as she opened the door.

"I've got a delivery for you, Miss Whitlock." He swallowed once and took a step back.

"Thank you," she said, and dug in her pocket for the crumpled ones she'd shoved in there after buying a drink from the mercantile that morning. She handed the money to him and he ran off back to the bakery.

There was a little note attached to the basket that said, "*I'm just being neighborly.*" He didn't sign his name, but she found herself smiling anyway.

Beckett sent something new every day. Scented candles for the store. Bath salts she could use to soak in after a long day at work. A bouquet of stargazer lilies and tulips he must've paid a fortune for since it was freezing outside. Chocolate covered strawberries. They were all accompanied with the same note—*I'm just being neighborly.*

And damn him for it. She hadn't been able to get him out of her head. It was far too easy to let those girlish fantasies come back to the surface. To bring back the taste of his lips against hers and the butterflies in her stomach as infatuation turned to something more.

He'd stopped by her house on a whim one evening as she was unloading groceries. He helped her unload them and then looked at her dishwasher for her when she'd mentioned it was making an odd sound. The sight of him in work-worn jeans and stripped down to his shirtsleeves as he tinkered with the dishwasher was enough to have her blood running hot. The artist in her could appreciate the muscles in his shoulders and arms as pure perfection. The woman in her wanted to take a bite out of him and damn the consequences.

If it wouldn't have looked completely ridiculous since it was the end of November and snow already covered the ground, she would've opened a window to cool things off a little.

She'd put away the groceries and they'd talked about his family and what was happening on the ranch, and when he was finished he put everything away, tested out the dishwasher, and then asked her if she wanted to grab a pizza and see a movie in the same tone of voice he used when talking about his cattle. Telling him no had been one of the most difficult things she'd ever done. But he didn't push. He just smiled and said she might change her mind tomorrow or the next day, so he'd keep asking.

That had been three days ago, and though she hadn't seen him again, his gifts continued to show up each day.

She barely heard the tinkle of the bells as her studio door opened. Beckett had made her lose her focus, and she found herself staring off into space, wasting time when she should've been working.

"My goodness, that's quite a frown you've got there," Mary MacKenzie said, closing the door behind her. "You'd think a woman being romanced like you are would be smiling like a fool."

"I'm not being romanced," Marnie said automatically. And then she shook herself out of her funk and took a good look at the woman who'd been more of a mother to her than her own.

Mary had always been larger than life in her mind. She was a petite woman, barely a couple of inches over five feet, and still beautiful in her bones. She kept her hair a pale shade of blonde and cut short around her triangular face, and she had it done like clockwork every two weeks. Her eyes were a softer shade than the MacKenzie blue, and she'd aged gracefully, the lines on her face adding interest and character instead of the despair that some women had over a few wrinkles. Her life was an active and blessed one.

It was amazing to think that big, strapping men like Cade,

Declan, Grant, and Shane had come from her. But she wasn't to be underestimated. The woman had a spine of steel and had ruled the MacKenzie clan with equal amounts love, affection, and discipline. No one got away with anything when Mary MacKenzie was watching. And when they did get away with it, it was because she let them.

If Marnie had had a camera in her hand at that moment she would've taken a picture of Mary. There was strength there. But behind the strength was a brokenness that couldn't lie to the camera.

Marnie went around the newly put together reception desk that Grant had worked his magic on and enfolded Mary in a hug to greet her. Mary clung a little longer than normal and Marnie let her. She wouldn't intrude and look to see what was wrong, but she'd listen if Mary wanted to tell her.

"I was wondering when you'd stop by," Marnie said.

"I've been meaning to," Mary said, pulling away and straightening her shoulders. No one else would know by looking at her that something was wrong. Only those who knew her well. "But I wanted to give you time to get things settled here. I know you like your space."

"I only like space from people I don't like. You don't count."

Mary laughed at that and pulled off her scarf and coat. Fresh snow clung to her lashes and hat, and her cheeks were rosy with the cold. It had been a lot of years since Marnie had experienced a winter with snow, and she'd only driven her van into a snow bank once. So far.

She'd had to purchase new clothes from the western store across the street—a jacket lined with lamb's wool, and thicker shirts and pants. And she finally got around to buying new gloves, and a hat and scarf as well. Not to mention the expense of snow tires. It had taken a precious chunk out of her savings, but there were dozens of deaths a year in their territory caused by hypothermia, and a good number of other people lost limbs from frostbite. It didn't pay to be stupid. Especially considering how much she worked outdoors.

The only good thing about the snow was it made a gorgeous backdrop for the family photos she'd started shooting. And curse

Lila or bless her, Marnie's calendar was full of work appointments and she'd already started bringing in income.

Marnie had insisted that the reception area of the studio be completed first. So many people walked by daily, looking in the windows and stopping to stare at the portrait displays she'd hung in the two picture windows that faced the street. They especially enjoyed the little display she called *People of Surrender*. She'd gotten permission from the subjects of course, but it thrilled people in the town to walk by and see their own faces, or the faces of someone they knew, immortalized in the window.

She wanted to make sure she gave a professional presentation from the start. She'd learned how important perception was in a professional setting. The people of Surrender might not remember her as a child, they might only know the rumors surrounding her gift, but they'd be intrigued enough to stop by and see for themselves. And she had no qualms about capitalizing on it.

The walls were painted a soft blue and the crown molding and trim was stained dark. Photographs were framed and hung on the walls—some from her personal collection of favorites and others of standard wedding and family portraits she'd done in the past. A dainty loveseat with a pattern in the same blue as the wall sat on one side, and a small tea table with two chairs sat on the opposite side. The pain in the ass reception desk sat right in the middle, facing the front, and blocked the door that had been added to lead back into the studio. The scratches that had been dug in when the studio had been vandalized had been sanded and stained, and they were only visible if you looked closely.

Marnie immediately grabbed the basket of cookies Beckett had sent and set it on the table.

"I've got hot tea if you'd like some," she said.

"That sounds perfect," Mary said. "It's bitter out today and dreary with it. I'm already tired of the snow and it's just started."

"It's been a long time since I've had a winter with snow. In the south, if there are even a few flurries, the whole city shuts down and people buy all the toilet paper and water from the shelves like it's the end times."

Mary laughed and the tightness in her face relaxed a little. "It'll take some getting used to, I imagine. Every year, James and I end up spending more and more time in warmer climates as soon as the newness of the first snow wears off. The cold is harder on the bones the older you get. He's already making noises about Hawaii after the New Year. The farm is taken care of between all the boys, and I'll be damned if I want to spend my golden years waking up before the roosters or running out to the barn, hip deep in snow because a cow's gone into labor."

Marnie's lips twitched. "Lying on the beach in Hawaii does sound more appealing." She brought two cups of tea and set them on the table, and then took the seat across from Mary.

"Nice basket of cookies you've got here," Mary said, arching a brow. "Not being romanced, you said?"

"He says he's being neighborly."

"Uh huh," she said, biting into a cookie. "I've been hearing how neighborly he's been from every shop in town he's visited. I also heard he fixed your dishwasher. Which," Mary said, pointing a finger at her, "is *our* responsibility as your landlords, so let us know if anything else goes wrong."

"Yes, ma'am." Marnie nodded and resisted the urge to salute.

Mary smiled and said, "I always knew you were a smart girl. Maybe the next time Darcy gets to town we should all take a girl trip. All my girls, and that includes you. Cade's wife, Bailey, has this lovely lingerie shop with the most beautiful things. You'll like Bailey. She's a real spitfire. And you'll like her friend Bianca too. We could all go shopping and have a spa day. Maybe by that time you'll be ready to shop for some lingerie."

Mary arched a brow and Marnie felt the heat in her cheeks. "I don't know. I've never really done anything like that. I'm not used to being around a lot of women."

"These are MacKenzie women. We're a whole different animal. I was married before. Did you know that?"

Marnie raised her brows in surprise. "No, I didn't."

"The folks around here have long memories, and they gossip about what happened a hundred years ago as much as they do about what happened last week, so you'll eventually hear it from someone."

"It's better than the news," Marnie agreed.

"Too bad it's not as reliable." Mary took a sip of tea and then settled in to tell her story. "I married Shane Nolan the year after I graduated from high school. Shane and James MacKenzie had grown up together and were best friends. And then they went off and joined the Marines together. I was a couple years behind them in school, and let me tell you, the summer after I graduated when Shane came home on leave, it was all I could do not to tackle him where he stood." Mary smiled and her eyes sparkled. "That would've been a real surprise to Shane because we didn't know each other all that well."

Marnie chuckled and settled into her chair. She'd missed adult conversation. She'd always been so careful not to forge new bonds or make new friends. Losing Darcy, her closest friend, had been like losing the best part of herself, and she hadn't been willing to go through that again.

Mary set down her teacup and grabbed a cookie. "Let me tell you, men are powerful creatures. If they only knew how powerful, every woman on earth would be in trouble. There's just something about a man who has that confidence in himself. Who can command with a look. Who doesn't have to speak to be heard. Looks don't seem to matter when a man has that kind of power. They're stubborn and hardheaded and have certain ideas about how they want things done. Shane Nolan had that in spades. And when he came back home on leave he'd bulked up a little too, with all the training. It wasn't until much later I found out he and James were both Special Forces and were in more danger than I could've imagined every time they left home.

"Girls flocked to Shane that summer. They weren't immune to that raw sex appeal just as I wasn't. But just like those kind of men have power over women, there are certain kinds of women who have power over those kind of men."

Mary winked and bit into another cookie. "I've been told a time or two that I'm stubborn and hardheaded and like things my own way. And even at eighteen years old, I knew the way to catch the interest of a man like Shane wasn't to tart myself up and flock around him like the other girls. I kept my distance."

Marnie's confusion must've shown on her face because Mary said, "Oh, I made sure I was in his path every now and again. He couldn't think of me all the time if I didn't give him a small glimpse of what he was missing, now could he? I'd make eye contact and give a friendly smile. Then I'd turn around and walk in the other direction." Her laugh was full of humor and good memories. "Lord, I drove him crazy."

"What happened?" Marnie asked, her curiosity piqued.

"Oh, men like Shane aren't ones to let moments pass them by. I was driving my daddy's pickup truck home one afternoon and I got a flat tire. Our house was a good forty-five minutes outside of Surrender and there were no cell phones in those days. I was well and truly stuck until someone came along. And on that particular stretch of road I could've been waiting for days.

"To make matters worse, the sky opened up about that time and we had a torrential downpour. I had extra blankets in the truck, a book, and two sacks full of groceries I could eat if I was there too long, though I knew if it got dark my parents would come looking for me. So I hunkered down and waited. And not twenty minutes later, along comes Shane, his headlights glaring into the cab of the truck when he pulled up behind me.

"There are moments in a woman's life she'll never forget," Mary said, her gaze turning nostalgic and a little bit sad. "And I knew the moment he knocked on the window in the pouring rain that that would be one of mine."

Her eyes got misty at the memory, even all these years later. And then her smile got big and a dimple fluttered in her cheek. "Well, I don't have to tell you what happened. As soon as he got into the truck the temperature in there went up about a hundred and fifty degrees. He was my first lover and what we had between us was so strong I didn't even notice that I should be uncomfortable that first time. We were like two animals tearing at each other. And all I could think was how much I wanted to do it again." She chuckled and her cheeks pinkened slightly. "Shane told me we were going to get married as soon as we could get a license because he had no plans to stop taking me to bed.

"And I can tell you, there's something even more amazing that happens when two people come together like that who are stubborn and strong-willed and have that dominant personality. There's nothing quite like it when you meet your match in every way and then learn to bend and compromise because their needs are more important than your own."

"Finding someone like that is rare," Marnie said. "You're very lucky."

"Even luckier because I found it twice. Shane and I hadn't been married but a few months when a couple of uniformed men showed up on my doorstep. James was with them and I could see he'd been terribly wounded. But we weren't close then. He was just the best friend of my husband, and it was hard for me to focus on anything other than the fact that they were telling me Shane was dead. And there I was, not even twenty years old, pregnant, and a widow. I couldn't imagine living a life without Shane in it, and I was devastated."

A tear trickled down Mary's cheek, but she didn't wipe it away. "It wasn't long after that I lost the baby too. The doctor said the shock and stress were just too much for my body to take. I didn't think I'd ever recover from that. She was a girl, and she was the only part of Shane I had left. It was like having him die all over again, and I wasn't sure I could survive another loss."

To see the woman who'd always been so strong show this vulnerability made Marnie feel useless and inadequate. "I'm so sorry, Mary."

"You know what?" she asked, pulling a handkerchief out of her bag and drying her face. "You've been a daughter to me from the first time Darcy dragged you to the house. Poor little thing. Scabs on your knees and dirty clothes, all that beautiful hair a tangled mess. And then I looked into those sad brown eyes of yours and I just fell in love. Pure and simple."

It was Marnie who felt the tears prick at her eyes now and she looked away, remembering all too well the little girl she'd been.

"I'm going to give you some advice, just like I would a daughter, because that's what you'll always be to me and I don't care who tries to say otherwise."

The tone was so matter-of-fact and such a one-eighty of their previous discussion that Marnie had to laugh.

"People like you and me are survivors, Marnie. The past is what shapes us. What makes us who we are. But it doesn't define you. It took James three years to wear me down. To pull me out of my own grief and misery so I could see what was staring me in the face. We all get second chances. And third chances. And fourth. But we have to be aware enough to recognize them when they come. Otherwise you miss out.

"Thank God that man was patient and kept wearing me down," she said. "I'd embraced my sadness like a shroud, and I didn't want anyone trying to take it from me. But the thing about the miseries of the past is that no matter how we might want to cling to them, the distance grows farther and farther away. The memories will always be there. And that's good. That's how we learn. But they'll never be our future again."

"Is that your way of telling me I should give Beckett a chance?"

"I'm telling you that you're loveable, Marnie. James loved me despite myself. Don't get in the way of your own happiness."

"Is that what you think I'm doing?"

"Partly," she said, nodding. "But I can also understand the need to protect yourself. Just because I lost you so many years ago didn't mean I didn't try to find you. I hope you know that James and I fought tooth and nail to get the state to agree for you to come live with us. We didn't know how bad it was at home for you. I knew money was tight, so we always offered your mama a little extra work when we could since she was probably the one trying to take care of bills and put groceries on the table. I had a feeling your daddy had a hard hand, and I looked for marks on your body every time you came over."

Marnie stared hard into the bottom of her teacup. "I didn't come over unless I was healed all the way. And I learned to stay out of his way for the most part the older I got."

"My poor baby," Mary said, letting the tears flow freely. "I'm so sorry we couldn't save you."

Marnie cleared her throat and held tight to the other woman's hand. "I'm back now. That's all that matters."

"And maybe you'll one day be comfortable enough to tell me about the sadness you brought back with you. I know you left a relationship to come back home. That's never easy."

"Easier than it should've been," Marnie said and then changed the subject. "You named Shane after your first husband?"

"James insisted," she said. "I was hesitant at first, but he eventually convinced me it was the right thing to do. We both loved Shane, and I had to remind myself that James lost a lifelong friend and someone who'd watched his back on the battlefield. They were as close as two friends could be, and James didn't openly grieve for Shane like I did. But he grieved all the same. If I'd been the shoulder he'd needed earlier on and not so consumed with my own grief we could've healed together. It's one of my biggest regrets.

"But naming our Shane after him was the right thing to do. He very much reminds me of my first husband. Stubborn as a mule and always a hero." Her smiled wavered and she looked down at her hands that gripped the teacup tightly. "I thought we'd lost him in that explosion. But my biggest fear is that we might still lose him. Stubborn as a mule," she repeated.

Marnie stayed silent because her visions that involved Shane were hazy. She couldn't tell Mary that his future was secure, and it was best not to give false hope. She'd learned that the hard way.

"One of the things I've always admired about you is that you never give up," Marnie told her. "Shane needs your strength. He needs his family, but he especially needs you. And whoever Lacy is. He needs her too."

"His physical therapist," Mary said, nodding. "They fight like cats and dogs. She's as stubborn as he is, thank goodness. I told him he'd met his match and there was no way he was going to intimidate a woman who'd done surgery in the middle of a battlefield." Mary straightened her spine and said, "I've taken up too much of your work day already. It'll be dark soon and I don't like to drive at night."

"I'm glad you stopped by," Marnie said, feeling much too formal all of a sudden.

She helped Mary with her coat and belongings and then left her hand on her shoulder until the other woman met her eyes.

"You said that I was like a daughter to you. I just want you to know that you and James were always the parents I wish I'd had. When Darcy and I went off to camp every summer, we told everyone that my last name was MacKenzie and we were sisters. Those were the best weeks of my life."

"Well, there goes my makeup." Mary pulled her into a hard hug and sobbed into her neck. And it wasn't long before Marnie realized she was crying too. She didn't know how long they stood there, but when they were finished, there was a lightness in her heart that hadn't been there before.

"Come to dinner tonight when you're done here," Mary said. "We've always got plenty of food."

"I'll take a raincheck. I think I'm going to have other dinner plans tonight."

"Good for you, my girl. Good for you. Maybe if you're lucky you'll get to have breakfast too." Mary chuckled and waved goodbye, the little bells above the door tinkling behind her.

Chapter Fourteen

Big Sky Ranch was one of the oldest operations in the state of Montana, and it had always belonged to a Hamilton. Now it belonged to Beckett.

They didn't have as much land as the MacKenzies. Not yet anyway. With the purchase of the Caldwell land it would put them darn close. The MacKenzies had shifted their operation so they ran and bred as many horses as they did cattle, so they had need for the extra acreage. The Hamiltons would always be cattlemen.

There was something about the land—owning it and working it—that soothed his soul like nothing else could. Just standing on the hill that overlooked the family home—his home now—and the vast pastureland and fences filled him with such pride he almost burst with it.

The fields were a blanket of white due to the fresh snow that had started falling at dusk. They'd get several feet before morning and the wind had already picked up. The weathermen hadn't called for a blizzard, but Beckett had lived and breathed Montana since his birth, and if a blizzard wasn't coming then it was the closest thing to it. Enough that an emergency alert had gone out warning that local businesses would be closed the next day and that everyone should stay off the roads.

The thing about a working ranch was that the animals didn't care that a blizzard was coming. The cattle still had to be fed and milked twice a day. Calves were getting ready to drop at any time and they had to make sure the mothers were checked regularly.

There were also pigs and chickens, not to mention horses. And when bad weather came, they all had to be rounded up and penned. It was an exhausting trial every blasted time. Because the animals seemed to sense the change in the weather and wanted to do their best not to cooperate.

He'd been right in the middle of pushing obstinate cows into the barn when his cell phone buzzed. He almost ignored it, and probably should have as he and his men had a limited amount of time to finish the job before the weather worsened. But he pulled it from the holster at his belt and recognized Marnie's number. His first thought was that something bad had happened. What other reason would she have to call?

But she'd surprised him. She'd always been very direct. There was never any guessing with Marnie. It was a refreshing experience. Hell, even when he'd been a nineteen-year-old kid he'd recognized it as a quality to appreciate. So when she'd asked if they could have dinner he'd only been stunned speechless for a moment.

"I tell you what," he'd said, putting his shoulder into the rump of a cow to get it moving. "Lock up now and come out to the ranch. The snow's coming faster and you're not used to driving in it. By the time you get here I'll be finished up with the evening feeding and ready for a shower and a meal."

She agreed as if they'd just made a casual business transaction and disconnected, leaving Beckett smiling into the phone.

"Boy, didn't I tell you to stay away from women?" his father said. "They ain't nothing but trouble. Didn't you learn anything from the last go-around?"

Carson Hamilton was in his mid-sixties and still worked the ranch with the enthusiasm of a much younger man. His dark blond hair was silvered at the temples and the lines on his face were from years of working in the sun. He was tall like his son, but his eyes were a piercing blue instead of gray. The gray had come from Beckett's mother.

"You also told me that I needed to get out and live beyond the ranch. That that's where I'd get life experience."

"That was when you were in college," he said, rolling his eyes. "Besides, when have you ever listened to me?"

"I always listen. I just don't always implement. Don't worry,

Pop. This woman is worth the trouble."

"Hmmph. I take it from what I overheard that you're not going to show up on our doorstep tonight to mooch dinner."

"You'd be right about that. Marnie Whitlock," he said by explanation.

His father slapped a cow on the rump and stared at him a few seconds. "Whew, boy. Talk about trouble. And it'll do nothing but follow her around her whole life. She's got the curse."

"She's got a gift," Beckett corrected. "And she's helped a lot of people with it. Don't judge her by her father."

Carson spat on the ground at the mention of Harley Whitlock. "Don't see how anything good could come from that man. A liar, a thief, and a murderer. A real bastard through and through. He's the only person I could ever say I was glad he was dead. And that he suffered when dying. You reap what you sow."

"And his daughter paid the price," Beckett said. "A lot of times at the hand of her father. She's a survivor. And she's made a good life for herself. She's back home now and it doesn't look like she plans on going anywhere."

"You were always stuck on her," Carson said. "It worried your mama sick when you started mooning over that girl. She was scared to death you were going to get her pregnant and then Harley would be tied to all of us. Maybe try to get part of the ranch as payment or restitution."

Beckett stopped cold and stared at his father, his hands on his hips. "You never said a word."

"Because we didn't have to. We didn't raise a fool. You've always been very respectful and private about your relationships. We would've heard otherwise if you hadn't been. And that's the way we raised you to be. You spent a couple years pining after that girl until you found your gumption to make a move. You're a slow one. Like to think things through first before you take action. You got that from me. Your mama has a quick temper and is a little high strung at times."

His father winked and pulled off his work gloves, sticking them in the back pocket of his insulated overalls. "That's what I love about her. She always keeps things interesting. And then once we saw what he'd done to you that night..." Carson shook his head and moved toward the big sliding doors of the cattle barn. "Your face was so swollen and your jaw busted up. God, I thought your mama was going to hunt him down with her shotgun and fill him full of buckshot. I was of the mind to let her too, but after we called the sheriff and learned they were already after him all we could do was wait and see."

"I don't remember a lot of what happened after he punched me that first time. Bastard had huge hands and it hurt like a bitch. I could hear Marnie screaming in the background, but the blood was rushing in my ears and my vision was blurry. I couldn't stop him."

"And that's nothing to be ashamed of," Carson said. "You were still more boy than man, and let me tell you, there's not many men who could stand up to Harley the way you did and live to tell the tale."

Beckett made a noncommittal sound. He'd always blamed himself for not being able to do more to stop Harley. And it had taken him a lot of years to realize there was nothing more he could've done. You couldn't stop crazy.

"It never occurred to me that there's a reason I've never had the interest for a long-term relationship. No matter how hard I tried I could never find another woman that's made me feel like Marnie does. It's always been her. From the very beginning. The timing wasn't right for us then. We were too young. And if Harley hadn't stopped us that night, he would've eventually been a problem. The best thing for everyone that night was when he drove over that cliff. It set us all free."

"I'm just telling you to be careful. Harley might be gone, but the girl still has trouble. I kept up with her enough through the years to know that that gift she has can be just as much of a curse. Not all the cases she helped on were successful. There were people who didn't get saved."

"It's not a magic trick," Beckett said, aggravated. "I don't know how it works as she's never explained it to me, but I don't think it's something she can always control. There were a lot more people she saved than she didn't. She can't save everyone. It's not her job to. People still have choices that can change the direction of anyone's future."

"You seem to know a lot about it."

"You weren't the only one who kept up with her over the years. I tried to read everything I could about her. Interviews she gave, and police statements. I never stopped loving her. Not even after she was taken away. But I also knew she deserved to get to live a normal life. That life wasn't here. At least not then. And my place will always be here."

"But now she's back," his father said.

"Now she's back," Beckett agreed.

They moved outside and closed the doors, leaving the animals to their evening meal and the warmth of the barn, and then they got on their horses and headed to the other barn to check on the other animals.

Beckett pulled up his balaclava and covered the bottom half of his face and then pulled his ski cap low over his ears. Then he pulled the hood of his jacket over that. The wind was bitter and slapped at the upper half of his face as he rode side by side with his father.

They rode in silence to the smaller barn on the west side of the property to check the horses, but the hands had already made sure they were in their stalls and settled and fed for the evening. Big Sky had a good team and things ran smoothly, but part of that was because Beckett, and his father to a certain extent, were always right in the middle of things. No one would care about their business like they did.

Beckett started to dismount to double check that things were as they should be—it wasn't unheard of for animals to escape because of someone's careless actions—but his father stopped him.

"I'll see to things here," Carson said. "You go ahead on up to the house and get ready for your company. You smell like the back-end of a cow."

"It's hard to refuse an offer as good as that one. Y'all have everything you need for the storm?"

"We're all set. And your mother has stew simmering on the stove and cornbread for supper, so I'm ready to get back myself. I won't be but a few minutes here."

Beckett nodded at his father and then dismounted his horse and handed over the reins so he could be put up with the others.

"You take the four-wheeler back," Beckett said. "I want to

stretch my legs."

It wasn't a long walk, but it was dark by the time the house came into view. When his father had decided to retire and put the ranch in Beckett's hands, his parents had moved out of the big house on the hill, as was tradition when the ranch passed to the next generation. Beckett had tried to get them to reconsider. He didn't need a house that big. But they'd insisted and had built a smaller house right on the lake about a mile past the cattle barn.

The main house had been built in the twenties from the proceeds gained during a successful stint at moonshining—a two-story log cabin with a shaker shingle roof and a porch that wrapped the entire way around the house. Large, rough logs were used as supports for the porch and snow covered the railing.

He'd always thought of it as a log cabin on steroids. There were huge windows front and back so light went all the way through the house, and a double staircase was showcased in the center, leading to two separate upstairs wings. Even as a child it had been too much room for just the three of them. But it was home. And more importantly, it felt like home.

It wasn't one of those houses where you couldn't sit on the furniture or where quiet was expected. He and his friends had tracked in muddy boot prints, the furniture had been well lived on, the floors scuffed, and an upstairs window broken from a poorly calculated game of indoor baseball.

He'd forgotten to call the house and let Izzy know he was having company for dinner. She'd been a staple at Hamilton House since long before he was born, and she'd decided to stay after the ranch had been passed to him. She said Master Beckett needed her a lot more than his parents did. And he thanked God every day she was there, because the house would probably fall in shambles around his ears without her.

Izzy oversaw the cleaning, cooked his meals, and she'd boxed his ears on more than one occasion growing up. And she looked like she wanted to box his ears right now.

"What do you mean you're having company over for dinner?" Izzy asked, brandishing a wooden spoon like some would a sword.

Isadora Blackstone was a little sprite of a woman with coal black eyes and hair to match—though the hair had a little help from

Clairol every few weeks. Her skin was the color of creamed coffee and her face was mostly smooth of wrinkles, due to the fact that she'd slathered it with Oil of Olay for more than fifty years. Her eyebrows were drawn on sharply with a black pencil and her lips were ruby red. She was maybe ninety pounds soaking wet, but when she got her dander up she was as scary as any giant.

"You think food just magically cooks itself and appears on your plate? Cooking for company takes planning and time. Especially if it's a lady friend. You've got to make a good impression. Unless it's that Hazel Trout. I'm not cooking for that little tramp, so if you're thinking of parking your horse in that particular barn you'd better think again."

Beckett snorted out a laugh before he could help himself and the spoon missed the tip of his nose by an inch. He congratulated himself on not flinching.

"I told you to stay away from that girl. I said, 'Master Beckett, you keep your dallying with that girl out of my house. She sees herself as Queen Bee over Big Sky Ranch, and I'm already Queen Bee. There ain't room enough for the both of us.' Didn't I tell you that?"

"Yes, ma'am," Beckett agreed quickly. She had told him that straight out, and he wasn't going to argue. Everyone knew that Izzy ruled the roost at Big Sky.

She nodded sharply and stuck her head in the refrigerator, slapping items on the counter.

"Shoo," she said. "Get out of my kitchen. You smell like you've been rolling in manure."

"Pretty close," Beckett said. "You'd think the cows would be smart enough to come in from the cold on their own."

"Thank goodness they're not. Otherwise, I wouldn't have steak thawed out and ready to put on the grill for your dinner guest. Now go, before you stink up the whole house. I used the Pine-Sol today on the floors and I like to keep the lemon smell as long as I can."

"I'm going," he said, and grabbed an apple from the bowl to take with him while her back was turned.

Izzy's bark was always worse than her bite, and by the time he was finished in the shower and dressed in jeans and a soft gray sweater that matched his eyes, the meal was cooked and warming in the oven until Marnie arrived. Izzy had made herself scarce, but left a note taped to the oven to remind him to be a gentleman and that she was going to bed for the evening because her reality TV show was on. She lived in the small guesthouse behind the garage.

When the doorbell finally rang, he let out a breath he hadn't realized he'd been holding. He hadn't really thought Marnie would actually come.

He hurried to open the door and then stared in surprise at the woman that stood on his doorstep. Her face was white as a sheet and she looked like she'd been rolling in the snow. White flakes crusted her from the top of her hat all the way to the top of her boots.

"What happened? Are you okay?" He reached out to pull her inside and he was surprised when she didn't pull away from his grasp. She must've been in shock. Or frozen solid.

"I didn't realize the weather was going to get so bad so quickly." Her teeth chattered and he steered her toward the fireplace and the blazing logs that burned there. "I tried to call you and cancel, but I couldn't get through. I think service is down. I didn't want you to think I'd driven in a ditch somewhere and have you go out and look for me."

"That's very thoughtful of you," he said, mouth twitching. "Did you walk here? I've never seen someone covered in this much snow from driving a car."

"The windshield wipers on my van decided to stop working. I had to roll down the window so I could see where I was going. And then when I parked and got out of the van the wind blew my door open hard and I couldn't get it shut again. When I pushed on it the wind decided to start blowing the other direction and it blew the door closed and me face first into the snow that built up next to the driveway." She went to wipe the snow from her face and remembered she had her gloves on, so she peeled them off and laid them in front of the fire. "At least I think I parked in the driveway. It might be the middle of your front lawn for all I know."

"I'm not sure I've ever heard you say that much at one time before. You must be thirsty."

"You make me nervous."

He burst out laughing at that. She'd told him that once before while on a certain Ferris wheel ride.

"Hand me your things and I'll hang them up to dry. There's fresh coffee or wine if you like."

"I don't drink," she said.

"Anything at all? Or just drinks of the alcoholic variety? I'm not a doctor, but I am a cattleman, and I know that my cows have to have water to survive."

"Are you comparing me to a cow?"

"It didn't start out that way in my head," he said, smiling sheepishly. "Maybe we should start over. Did you have a pleasant drive?"

Her mouth quirked and her eyes sparkled with laughter. Color was coming back into her cheeks and the tension went out of her body. "It was a lovely drive. Very picturesque. I would've taken pictures if my lens cap hadn't frozen to the camera."

"That's nice then," he said, hanging up her outerwear close to the fire. "Can I interest you in a beverage of the non-alcoholic sort?"

"I'll stick with water for now. I've been told it's a necessity for survival."

"Whoever told you that was a genius. You should stick with him."

"Only if he feeds me soon. It's cruel to make a person smell something that delicious and not feed them."

"Like the smell?" he asked, a wicked glint in his eye. "Izzy got a new air freshener. It always smells like steak in here. Sorry to disappoint you."

"Oh, well. Like I said, I only wanted to come by and tell you I wouldn't be stopping by for dinner. I'll be lucky to make it home at all if I don't leave now."

"Don't be ridiculous. I'm not letting you drive home on an empty stomach with no working windshield wipers. That would make me a cad."

"I'd hate to damage your reputation."

"My reputation has taken plenty of licks lately and managed to survive. And I hate to break it to you because I know you were hoping to ditch me tonight so you could run home and curl up with a good book, but you are well and truly stuck here for a little while.

But I do promise to feed you and I promise to keep you out of the wine no matter how much you beg me to open a bottle."

She looked at him out of serious eyes, her full lips still curved in a soft smile. "If I'm stuck, I'm stuck. Looks like I'm staying."

The spit in Beckett's mouth dried up and he had trouble swallowing. It wasn't the words she said, but the way she'd said them. Her voice had gone husky and there was something in the way she looked at him that told him she'd known exactly where she'd end up for the night.

He arched a brow and said, "You knew all along you'd be staying the night here."

"I also know that the steak in the oven will keep a good long while."

"You're going to have to tell me exactly what point you're trying to get across, Marnie. I'm not as good as you are at reading minds."

"I know. And I won't read yours. I can promise you that."

"It's probably best you didn't. I've been trying to figure out what you've got on under that bulky sweater since you took your coat off."

"I didn't have to read your mind to know that. You scare the hell out of me, Beckett Hamilton."

"That kind of takes the edge off the foreplay we had going there. I don't want you scared. I want you turned on."

She laughed until tears rolled down her cheeks, and she dropped down into one of the overstuffed chairs in front of the fireplace.

"I remember you always being on your best behavior with women, even when I was a sixteen-year-old girl. You were a gentleman. What happened to that?"

"I feel overly comfortable with you. And I want you a lot more now than I did when you were sixteen. I've waited for you for fifteen years. I figure if I'm not direct it'll be another fifteen years before you let me kiss you again."

"It was a good kiss," she said, smiling.

"I've regretted every day since that I didn't start kissing you sooner."

"The timing of it didn't matter. We would've ended up in the same place if Harley hadn't come along."

His lips pressed together and he went stone still.

"No, don't blame yourself," she said, getting up and crossing over to him. "There's no reason pretending like the past didn't happen. It's something between us and we've got to both live with it. It's part of the reason I kept telling you no all these weeks."

He nodded. "I figured as much. I couldn't protect you then. Why would you think anything had changed now that you're back?"

"No, you've got the wrong reason altogether. I told you no because I very much remember that kiss and what I felt like when I was with you. I knew where we were headed, even if you didn't completely know. I saw us together. Under a willow down by the lake."

He nodded and said, "There's a big willow a couple of miles from here along a secluded trail. I used to ride there when I was younger when I wanted to think. It was my thinking place."

"You would've taken me there," she said. "And I would've let you with all the trust and innocence a sixteen-year-old girl could have. I would've let you kiss me and love me and more. And we would've kept sneaking back there because we wouldn't have been able to get enough of each other."

"That doesn't sound like a good reason to keep telling me no all these weeks. It sounds like a reason to say yes. We could've been under that willow when there was still grass beneath us instead of snow. It's going to be damned cold now."

She laughed and he grinned at her response. "What I'm saying is I needed to say no to make sure I could. I was in a relationship for a couple of years."

"I know," he said. "I saw the articles in the paper. You looked happy."

"Not happy in the relationship. But happy in my career and fulfilled. He played off that. And I let him because for the first time in my life I was getting to do exactly what I loved and making a good living from it. I needed space from that after I came here."

"I can understand that. It takes time to move on after you close a certain door in your life."

"I spent a lot of years in therapy, you know," she said.

"I'm glad. I can't imagine what it must've been like for you growing up. And that you were able to hide it from all of us."

"At first I thought maybe if I'd been born different he wouldn't have had a reason to beat me."

"Some people don't need a reason. He would've found a reason one way or another."

"That's what my therapist said," she said, nodding. "He was just a bad person. There's no cure for that. And it took me a while to admit to myself that part of me was glad the MacKenzies hadn't been able to adopt me, even though I felt broken without them in my life. Even though I hated leaving you before we'd ever had a chance to get started."

"Why were you glad?" he asked.

"Because for as long as I could remember my one goal was to have freedom. From my father and from Surrender. I was counting down the days until I could leave. I needed to know that I could survive on my own. And once I'd survived on my own I needed to discover that I hadn't deserved what he'd done to me. I'm so fucked up, Beckett. Why would you want that?"

"Everyone's got baggage, Marnie. Some more than others. But I'm sure your therapist also told you that having baggage doesn't keep you from having the right to happiness. But you've got to play a part in finding that happiness."

"I thought that's what I was doing with Clive. I'd spent time on my own. Worked my way across the country and finally started a business of my own. I was ready for an adult relationship. I had it all. And then I found myself back in a situation where I was walking on eggshells all the time. The only thoughts in my head were doing things to please him so he'd be happy with me."

The look on his face must've alerted her to his thoughts because she hurriedly said, "He wasn't physically abusive," she assured him. "He never hit me. But he controlled me. He owned me. But in the opposite way of my father. My father was always ashamed of my gift. He hated it and hated me because I had it and he didn't. Clive was the opposite. He loved my gift. Loved that it brought attention to him and that his name was associated with mine. I was like a pet. And he never saw me as a woman or as someone of worth. And then I found out he'd forged papers so he was executor of everything I did. He literally owned me at that point, and I knew I had to get out before there was nothing left of me at all. I'm tired of being everyone's afterthought. Of being something they need or want to use."

"Wait a second," Beckett said. "This guy lied and stole from you, and you just walked off without a fight?"

She sighed. "I don't have a lot of fight left in me, Beckett. It was easier to walk away and start over. He can have what he wants. I've got my freedom again and that's all that's ever been important to me."

"You're crazy if you think a man like that is just going to let you walk away. I kept up with you over the years, Marnie. You're worth millions. And if he owns your work, he's going to keep coming after you for more because that's a cash cow that'll never dry up. Especially if you become a reclusive artist living in Nowhere, Montana, and your photographs become hard to find. Your prices will probably triple."

"I was never important enough to Clive for him to think I'd be worth chasing after. I promise he probably hasn't given me a thought since I walked out the door. He's got business all over the world. I'm sure he already has someone filling my place."

He shook his head at her naïveté. At her lack of self-worth. "Marnie, you're an amazing woman. You're smart and talented and you have a wit that can cut you off at the knees before you realize you're laughing. You're strong and stubborn and you're right where you're supposed to be. You just took a little detour on the way."

"I know that," she said. "I know this is where I'm supposed to be. I know that I'm brave and strong and that there's more to me than people see. I'm not just poor white trash from Nowhere, Montana. I came from that, though. That'll never change."

"Does it matter?" he asked.

"It shouldn't. It doesn't matter as much as it used to. No one in all the other places I've lived knew where I came from. I was just me. And still they looked at me like I was a freak of nature."

"They don't understand you. Most people don't understand when they see greatness. They're too small minded."

"I don't care about other people just now. I'm more interested in something else."

He recognized the change in her. She was done talking about

herself. About the past. The look in her eyes was unmistakable, and he was starting to wonder if maybe they were taking things too fast. Yes, it had been fifteen years. But she'd been back in Surrender less than two months. Neither of them were teenagers anymore, but there was so much more at stake now.

She took a step back and then grabbed the bottom of her sweater with both hands and pulled it over her head.

He'd guessed wrong. The bra she wore was lacy and the dark blue of a midnight sky. Her breasts weren't on the large side, but they swelled over the lacy cups and were high and round. She'd always been thin with delicate bones—fragile. Until you got to know her and realized the core of her was solid steel.

She leaned over to untie her boots and toed them off, all the while keeping her gaze on his, almost defiantly. All he could do was watch, mesmerized by her movements. When her fingers went to the button of her pants he finally got his wits about his and shook himself out of the stupor.

"Stop," he said and she froze where she stood. Embarrassment pinkened her cheeks and she looked down at the ground, her hands dropping to her side.

Beckett went to her then and lifted her chin so she was forced to look him in the eye. "I've dreamed of taking your clothes off for fifteen years. Don't take that pleasure away from me." And then he kissed her before she could argue with him.

It was like the first time. But different. Her lips held the same shape and her taste was the same, but this wasn't a kiss of innocence as it had once been. Those days were long gone. This was a kiss of longing and passion—years of built-up need.

She wanted him. The way she trembled in his arms wasn't from fear, but excitement. Or maybe he was the one that trembled.

"Beckett," she whispered. "Please take me to bed. Or here. Anywhere. I can't wait."

"The bed," he said, kissing her throat. "It has to be the bed this time."

His muscles strained as he told himself to go slow when the urge was to throw her over his shoulder and race up the stairs to his room. His heart pounded in his chest and her kisses became impatient—ravenous. She tugged at his sweater and pulled it over his head. He didn't see where it landed. Didn't care.

All he knew was that his mouth belonged fused to hers. Her fingers spread across his chest and her hands moved around to his back, pulling him closer. He began moving her backward toward the stairs, toeing off his shoes while his fingers found the clasp of her bra. She let it slide down her arms and drop to the ground, and then they were skin to skin and he thought nothing had ever felt as good.

"I can't make it any farther," she said. "Please." Her fingers tugged at the button on his jeans and he breathed a sigh of relief when she got them undone and was pushing them down his hips. His cock was so hard it hurt and all he wanted was to be inside her. He'd waited this long. He could wait the few minutes it took to get upstairs to the bedroom.

To speed things along he shucked his jeans where he stood so he was completely naked, and then he hitched her up so her legs wrapped around him. He couldn't stop kissing her. Touching her. He made it halfway up the stairs before he had to stop and taste the sweet buds of her nipples. Her back arched over the banister and he took a pink bud in his mouth, suckling gently until she writhed in his arms.

Her hips moved against him and he could feel the heat of her pussy through her jeans against his cock. He rocked against her as he suckled, and then he switched sides and paid attention to the other breast. Her fingers speared into his hair and pressed him tighter against her, and her mewls of pleasure grew louder.

He let go of the nipple with a wet *pop* and then grabbed hold of her, carrying her to the landing. He let her go so her feet touched the floor and his fingers went to the snap of her jeans. She helped him push them down and he briefly saw the matching navy panties that barely covered her before he pushed those down too.

"Hurry," she whispered as he backed her toward the door of his bedroom. "Hurry, hurry."

"No," he managed to get out. "I want to see you. All of you. We've waited too long to hurry now."

She growled in frustration and his shoulder hit the doorframe as they circled into the room. Her teeth nipped into his shoulder and her leg hooked around his hip, searching for him. She was wet.

God, she was wet. He could feel her desire. Her need. But he didn't give in and plunge into her as he wanted. Instead he picked her up and made it the rest of the way into the room, dumping her on the bed unceremoniously.

She laughed as he came down on top of her. And then the laugh turned into a moan as he kissed his way down her body, savoring the taste of her. He could smell the light scent of lemons from the soap she used. And the musk of her desire as he settled between her thighs.

Her hands grasped the covers and her breath came in short pants. Her folds were slick and creamy and her clit was swollen with need, and when his mouth latched onto the taut bud her hips arched and she let out a long, low moan of pleasure.

* * * *

"What?—" Marnie gasped. "What are you doing?"

She'd never been more mortified in her life. She wasn't experienced when it came to sex. Clive had never done any more than he'd had to when they'd been intimate, and she'd always thought of sex as more of a "man's sport." She'd had no idea that something like this was even possible.

"I'm making you come," he said. His hands held her ass up and he fed on her like a starving man at a banquet. He suckled and licked, and then his tongue did something indescribable and rockets exploded behind her eyelids. She didn't realize she'd screamed out her orgasm. She only knew she'd never felt anything like what she'd just experienced.

The only orgasms she'd ever had were ones she'd given herself or the spontaneous ones she experienced during an erotic dream. She'd never been able to come with Clive, but she'd always read that was normal with a lot of women, so she hadn't thought much of it. Once they were finished with sex she either went to sleep or went into the bathroom and finished the job herself. He'd never noticed. She'd never known what she'd been missing.

"Can you do that again?" she panted.

"Many times." The room was dark and she heard him rummage around in the bedside table and then curse.

"What's wrong?" she asked.

"Condom. They're in there somewhere."

She stopped him with her hand and wrapped a long leg around his hip. "I'm on the pill. Please, I want to feel all of you."

"Jesus, Marnie," he said, his breath seeming to explode from him. "I won't last ten seconds with nothing but skin between us."

"I've got faith in you. Nothing between us, Beckett. Please."

She felt him shift in the dark as he settled himself between her thighs. His chest hair rasped against her nipples and he kissed her again, this time softer—gentler. His tongue slid against hers and she tasted herself—sweet and salty at the same time. Then she felt his hand between them as he guided himself to her opening.

And then she felt the fullness of him as he pressed against her. He was big and her breath caught as he stretched her like she'd never been stretched before. He took his time and let her adjust, continuing to kiss her as he kept a steady pressure while entering her.

Her nails bit into his back and her legs wrapped around his waist. It seemed to take an eternity before she felt him fully pressed against her. She was breathless. And then he grasped her hands in his and began to move. Her hips matched his thrusts and she felt the build inside her once again. Her dreams weren't comparable to the real thing. How could they be?

"Come on, baby. Come for me again," he whispered against her cheek.

Almost as if she'd needed the prompt, she felt herself fall over the edge. It was different this time. With his mouth it had been an explosion of light and sound—the flash and bang of intense pleasure. This time it was a symphony of color, a slow roll of pleasure that consumed her from the inside out. She clenched around him and heard him moan against her neck as her muscles tightened and spasmed.

Sweat covered their bodies but he continued to move—faster and faster—so her orgasm rolled from one to the next—a continuous pleasure that had her gasping for breath. And then she felt him stiffen above her and the long, low groan as he spurted inside her.

She didn't know how long they lay there, holding each other.

Maybe they dozed. She wasn't sure. But when she felt him stir against her the sweat on her skin had cooled and she shivered. He was still inside her, soft now, but the connection was still there.

He kissed her and her hands traced the muscles of his back. She could touch him all day, so spectacular was his body. Then she noticed he wasn't so soft inside her anymore and chuckled.

"Can you do that again?" she asked, repeating her earlier question.

"I told you," he said. "Many times."

Chapter Fifteen

As Thanksgiving and Christmas passed, Marnie found that she and Beckett slipped into an easy routine. She'd been surprised by how comfortable she was with him. That she didn't mind when he stayed over and left some of his things lying around. And that she felt as at home at Hamilton House as she did at her own. She didn't feel like a second-class citizen or an imposter. She was Marnie Whitlock and she could be or do whatever she damned well pleased. It was an exhilarating discovery.

And it hardly bothered her at all that her visions had all but stopped. She could still read people if she wanted, or she'd get the occasional unwarranted glimpse into someone's future. But there were no more visions that took hold of her by the throat and showed her what was coming in her life or the direction she needed to go. She hoped that meant that everything was exactly as it should be.

Cooper had mentioned to both Hazel and Denny Trout that it was in their best interest to leave her and Beckett alone. The MacKenzies owned the little house Hazel and her mother lived in, and they also owned the place Denny rented since the Caldwells had always been too cheap to provide a house for their foreman. It had only taken a mention that if anything else happened, they'd both find themselves looking for another place to live.

Beckett had been true to his word. He had been able to do it many times. Many, *many* times. And when Darcy had come home for Christmas and they'd reunited, the first thing out of Darcy's mouth was, "Well, damn. The sex must be amazing. That smile won't leave your face."

Marnie had just arched a brow, but she hadn't disagreed with her friend. The sex was, in fact, amazing. She was insatiable. She'd told Beckett she had a lot of years to catch up on, so she hoped he was prepared. He seemed not to mind too much, though they'd had to get creative between her busy client schedule and calving season.

The MacKenzies had hired her to do a full shoot of their family. They wanted an intimate picture book to hand down to the next generations, including some of the old photographs of when the ranch had first been built, up to present day. It was a massive project, and Marnie was working on it in her spare time between weddings and other jobs.

She'd been driving at the MacKenzie Ranch one afternoon, and on a whim, she'd veered left and headed toward Hamilton land. She didn't know what had made her do it. But thoughts of him consumed her, especially since he'd left her sated and satisfied only that morning.

Luck had been on her side. She saw him from a distance nailing part of a fence back up, his horse tethered close by. She stopped and took a couple of pictures, loving the intensity on his face, the way his hands so skillfully used the hammer.

Snow still covered the ground, but he didn't seem bothered by the cold. She pulled the van up beside him and his horse snorted and took a few steps to the side.

"I was just thinking about you," he said as she hopped out of the van.

And just like that they were on each other. She didn't remember climbing into the back of the van or how he only got one leg of her jeans pulled off before he was inside her. It was a fast and furious coupling that only lasted minutes, but it was enough for the moment.

There'd been other times as well. When he'd stop into town for lunch or to pick up some supplies, he'd always swing by the studio to say hello. And if she wasn't busy they'd often find themselves in her little office with her sprawled across the desk, or in the tiny bathroom as he fucked her from behind and they stared at each other in the mirror. He treated her like a woman. And she loved it.

"What do you want, Marnie?" he asked. She'd sent her receptionist out for lunch.

She'd walked to the front door of the studio and locked it, but people could still see in if they looked through the glass. And then she'd pushed him to the floor behind the big desk and undone the snap to his jeans, pushing them down just past his hips. She'd left on his shirt.

His eyes widened in surprise as she took off her pants completely. She felt wild and free, and the thought of someone looking through the window and seeing them gave her an added surge of adrenaline.

"Marnie," he whispered. "Come here."

But she surprised him again. It was rare she felt bold enough to take charge. She was still unsure of herself in a lot of areas, but Beckett was a good and patient teacher. So when she turned around and knelt down so her pussy was positioned just over his face, she reveled when he said, "Oh, hell yeah." And then she leaned down to take his cock in her mouth.

His boots stuck out from the side of the desk, but anyone passing would have to look closely to notice. Even if they did notice, she didn't really care. His tongue was working a miracle on her clit.

"Fuck," he said. "I'm going to come. Ride me."

"No," she said around his cock. The muscles in his legs tightened and his mouth paused. And then he pulled her back down and brought her to a strong, hard orgasm just as she felt the rush of salty fluid in her mouth.

They'd barely gotten their clothes back on before her receptionist had walked up and rattled the door to be let back in. And then Marnie and Beckett had gone over to the diner for lunch like nothing out of the ordinary had happened.

But she should've known things were too good to last. The snow was still falling in late January, and she'd finished her last client for the day and was headed out to Hamilton House for the evening, her overnight bag beside her. She hadn't been quite brave enough to move in her things like Beckett had suggested.

They were good at it. Keeping things nice and easy between

them. Simple. There were no demands and they each had their freedom. And the more time she spent with him the more she realized that he didn't want to control her or use her in any way. He just wanted her.

The oak tree at the center of the fork in the road no longer brought her the pain it first had when she'd returned to Surrender. She drove past it without a thought, making her way to Hamilton House, and her cell phone rang. She didn't recognize the number, but that wasn't so uncommon.

"Captured Moments," she said by way of greeting. "This is Marnie."

"I'd thought for sure you'd have gotten over your little tantrum by now and come crawling back," Clive said.

Her foot lifted off the accelerator and the van crawled to a stop in the middle of the road. She grasped the phone tightly in one hand and the wheel with the other. Nausea rolled in her stomach. Beckett had been right. Clive wouldn't leave her alone. Not when he had so much to gain.

"Hello? Marnie? Are you there?"

"I'm here. What do you want?"

"Don't be ridiculous. It's time for you to end this farce and come home. I'm sure you've taken some lovely photographs while you've been staying in Bum Fuck Montana, but it's time to get back to the real world. I've got a show scheduled for you in New York at the end of May."

"I guess you'll have to cancel it," she said, the anger building inside of her. "I'm not doing any more shows. And last I checked, I'm not having anything more to do with you either."

"Unfortunately, that's not what our contract says."

"Not any contract that I signed."

"That doesn't matter. Who's going to believe you? Certainly not a court of law or the judges I play golf with every week."

"We're done, Clive. You can't have me."

"Stupid girl. I never wanted you. Your photographs and that amazing psychic ability, on the other hand, have made me a fortune. You don't think I just randomly walked into your studio that day, do you? It was just a fortunate circumstance that you happened to be a decent photographer with an inkling of talent that I could use to my advantage."

She pressed down on the accelerator and the van started forward again. "I'm sure that's fascinating," she said, her voice dead of all emotion.

She'd already known that of course, but the confirmation was still painful. Maybe she just wasn't the kind of person who was easy to love. Her parents hadn't loved her. And neither had Clive, even though he'd told her repeatedly that he did. But to him, they'd been empty words. The MacKenzies were the only ones who genuinely loved her, and she still had to wonder why. She didn't have anything to offer them in return.

"Stop pouting. I'll be there in a couple of days to collect you and any photographs you've taken over the last few months. And don't try to tell me you haven't been taking them. You can't go a day without lifting that camera to your face."

"You're not welcome here and I'm not going anywhere with you," she told him.

"Be ready and don't keep me waiting. I promise you won't like it if you do."

He hung up and she realized she was trembling. She had no idea what to do. But she only knew that the only way she'd be going anywhere with Clive Wallace was if he killed her first.

Chapter Sixteen

She'd almost gotten herself under control by the time she pulled into the driveway at Hamilton House.

It was just past five o'clock, and she knew Beckett would still be in the barn, overseeing the evening feeding and milking, so she at least had time to shower and get herself together before he noticed anything was wrong. But when she walked into the house, she was surprised to find company there.

"Marnie," Mary MacKenzie said, her face beaming in greeting.

Mary and James both hugged her, and then she received a hug from Beckett's mother, Judy, as well.

"I hope you don't mind, but James and I are crashing your party tonight for dinner."

"Of course I don't mind," Marnie said. "You're always welcome."

"We're leaving for Hawaii tomorrow morning for a couple of weeks. James finally talked me into getting out of this blasted snow. We're supposed to have another foot by the weekend."

Marnie groaned at the news. "That should make some of my outdoor photo shoots interesting."

"Are you feeling all right?" Judy asked, laying the back of her hand to Marnie's cheek.

Marnie had been nervous before meeting Beckett's parents the first time. She'd heard stories about Judy Hamilton. That she was a real hard charger and a ball buster at that. People either spoke of her with reverence and awe or pure terror.

But Judy had looked Marnie over once and said, "You look like good people to me." And then she'd hugged her and that had been that.

They didn't see each other often because Beckett's parents lived an active social life and they believed in giving their son his privacy and space. But Judy had always treated Marnie with a motherly air that surprised her.

"I'm okay," Marnie answered. "Just a bit of a headache I can't get rid of."

Judy and Mary both clucked like mother hens and Judy said, "Why don't you go up and rest a little before the boys get in from the barn? They'll be another half hour at least."

"I think I'll do that, thanks," she said, glad for the escape.

She retreated upstairs and fell face first into the bed she shared with Beckett, trying not to think of Clive and what she'd do when he showed up in Surrender. And he *would* show up. Clive didn't make empty promises.

She must have dozed for a while because she woke to the sound of the shower being turned off. Beckett came out of the bathroom with a towel wrapped around his waist and droplets of water clinging to his shoulders.

"Hey," he said, pulling underwear and a shirt from the drawer. "Mom said you weren't feeling good. You were out like a light when I came in."

"Just a headache. I feel better now."

She scooted off the bed and went into the bathroom, staring at herself in the mirror. She was pale and even she could see the strain and worry in her eyes. There was no doubt that Beckett would see it too.

She turned on the water and splashed the cool liquid over her face. And when she went back out to the bedroom Beckett was dressed.

"You don't have to come down for dinner," he said. "They'll understand if you're not feeling well. You still look pale to me."

"I'm fine," she said. "And I'd like to spend a little time with Mary and James before they leave. I haven't seen them since Christmas."

He smiled. "You would've seen them at the New Year's Eve

party they threw, but you distracted me with that little dress you had on before we could get there. I still have an imprint of the gearshift on my ass."

She tried to smile, but was afraid she was failing miserably, so she held out her hand instead and said, "Ready to go down?"

He looked at her strangely, but only nodded and took her hand in his.

Beckett's bedroom and bathroom, plus a game room, were the only rooms on the west side of the house. There was a big open loft and a railing that looked straight across to the rooms on the east side of the house, or straight down to the living area below.

"Marnie, wait," he said, stopping her and turning her to face him before they reached the stairs. They could hear laughter from somewhere down below, probably the kitchen as that was the place almost everyone liked to gather.

"I want to tell you something."

She looked at him and knew what he was going to say before he opened his mouth. It slammed into her and she almost stumbled under the intensity. He loved her. And after the phone call she'd just received from Clive, she couldn't bear for him to say the words. Because she knew he was only going to be hurt in the long run.

He opened his mouth to speak, but she threw herself at him, kissing him with everything she had. He caught her against him and met her mouth with his own. There was nothing sweet or gentle about this kiss. It was carnal and full of need and desperation.

She tore at the shirt he wore, pulling it from the waistband of his jeans, her nails raking across his taut abs. It was then she realized where she'd experienced this before. This was how the vision started she'd had so many months before—the one that constantly left her aching and wanting more.

* * * *

Beckett wasn't sure what had happened. He only knew that when he saw her standing there pale and looking a little lost, he'd had to tell her he loved her. He'd always loved her, and he'd known somewhere deep in his heart that she would always be the only woman for him. He'd known she'd have to return to Surrender someday, only because God wouldn't have been so cruel as to let them find love if He didn't mean for them to end up with each other.

But before the words could come out of his mouth, something came over her. Lust slammed into his body as her mouth fused to his, and all the blood drained from his head and straight to his lap. His cock went rock hard in an instant, and before he knew what she was about, her hot little hands had undone his belt, pushed down his jeans, and were wrapped tight around his dick.

Laughter wafted up from below and he tried to pull her back, farther from the railing so they wouldn't be seen if someone walked by below, but she stood her ground and squeezed him, her eyes glinting wild and wicked.

He must have lost his mind to strip her out of her clothes so she stood naked on the landing. But he was long past the point of rational thought. His clothes had disappeared somewhere along the way too and he held the length of her hair as he spun her around so her hands held tight to the railing.

She tugged against his hand and then looked at him over her shoulder, daring him to take her. And he lost complete control. He kicked her legs apart and thrust into her with one hard push. She gasped loudly and he clamped a hand over her mouth.

She bit his finger. Hard. But she was oblivious to what she'd done. Her muscles tightened around him and she was already coming. He slammed into her over and over again, a beast inside of him coming to the surface and claiming what was his.

The upper half of her body hung over the railing and he grabbed onto her breasts as he continued to fuck her with abandon. Tiny mewls escaped her lips with every thrust and he felt his balls draw tight as his orgasm drew closer. And then he pinched both her nipples and felt her tighten around him again.

Her muscles milked him, massaged him, and then he felt the liquid gush of her orgasm and barely got his hand over her mouth as she screamed out his name. Come exploded from his body and he jerked against her as jet after jet of semen coated her vaginal walls. It was like he'd stuck his cock into an electrical socket. The tremors seemed to last forever and he was wrung dry and exhausted by the time the last one came. And then he heard it.

"Beckett? Is that you?" his mother called out.

He heard her footsteps on the hardwood floor below and jerked Marnie back from the railing, pulling them both to the floor. If he hadn't been so tired and mortified at the thought of almost getting caught by his mother, he would've laughed. As it was, he looked at the woman trapped beneath his body and laid his forehead to hers.

Her eyes were closed but she rubbed his back soothingly.

"I love you, Marnie," he said.

Chapter Seventeen

Two days later Beckett was still wondering what he'd done wrong.

He'd told her he loved her. That was the natural progression of things. But by the way she'd reacted you would've thought he'd told her someone had died. She wiggled out from under him and crawled into his bedroom on hands and knees since there was a possibility his mother was still standing below.

She'd gotten dressed without a word, given him a fake smile, and then headed down to eat dinner with his parents and the MacKenzies. As if nothing life-altering had just taken place. Then she'd made an excuse of why she couldn't stay the night and hadn't answered his calls the next day.

He needed answers, and he was going to get them. He loved her. And he knew that she loved him too. They had too much between them—past, present, and future. The more he thought about it the more determined he was to get answers. Why didn't she realize they could be so much more together than apart? She still had her freedom. Her independence. But they could make something special together. She was just stubborn. And afraid. Loving him was a risk. But he liked to think he was worth it.

Two mornings after he'd last seen her, he got into his truck and headed to the house on the river to see her and get some answers. But when he got there, she was already gone for the day. So he turned around and drove the twenty-minute drive into town instead.

His cell phone rang about halfway there. "Hamilton," he said.

"Beckett, this is Mrs. Baker. There was an older gentleman in here early this morning. He checked in last night at the B&B and then came in for breakfast. He ordered a bran muffin and a black coffee. What people order says a lot about them, I always say."

"Yes, ma'am," he said. Beckett waited patiently for her to get to the point. He knew the cadence of conversation in Surrender. It was never fast and often meandering.

"Anyway, the reason I call is that this man was looking for Marnie. I know she doesn't open the shop until nine, so I told him he was a little early. But he was asking where she lived and where he could find her. I didn't say anything of course. Marnie's one of ours, you know. But I thought I should call and let you know. He seemed slimy to me, and I know Marnie will be at the studio any minute. He's been sitting in his car over at the B&B waiting for her."

A tightness settled in Beckett's stomach and his jaw clenched. "Thank you, Mrs. Baker. I appreciate the call. I'm almost to town myself."

"Oh, good. It's been a while since something exciting has happened down here. I'll let the customers know."

He had a feeling who the bran muffin was, and it just so happened Beckett was itching for a good fight. Reputation and propriety be damned. If the people wanted something to talk about, he was going to give it to them.

* * * *

Marnie had already put in a good two hours of work before she drove into the studio that morning. A couple had scheduled their engagement pictures at sunrise. Since that was a very small window of time, she'd been up and dressed with her equipment before dawn, out in the middle of nowhere in pristine snow with nothing but the mountains and the sunrise as her backdrop.

She was dog tired, and it hadn't helped that she'd had two sleepless nights. She missed Beckett beside her. She'd bungled everything. Both the way she'd reacted when he'd told her he loved her, and by not telling him about Clive's phone call. But God, she was ashamed. How was it that someone who had the ability to see other people's futures couldn't see a man like Clive for what he was?

She needed to see Beckett, to explain to him. She didn't have another appointment until later than morning and Jenny, her receptionist, would be there to answer the phones. So she turned in the direction of Hamilton House, hoping to find Beckett out in the barn. But when she got there the foreman had told her he'd left early that morning to run some errands, so she turned around and headed to town.

There was an open parking spot near the library, and thoughts of hot tea and a short nap in her office were prevalent in her mind. She stayed to the sidewalk and was past the sheriff's office before she saw him standing a few feet down from her studio.

"You're late," Clive said, straightening. "How are you supposed to run a successful business if you can't show up on time?"

She froze and fear crept up inside her. She hadn't recognized him. Months apart had put his image out of her mind, and now that she was face to face with him again, she wondered why she'd never really stopped to look at him before.

He was slick and smooth—like a politician—and you could see the breeding and money in the way he talked and carried himself. He wasn't her type. Maybe that's why she'd let him sweet talk her. Or maybe he'd been that good of an actor.

"I manage somehow," she forced out. She saw Jenny sitting at the reception desk in the studio, her eyes wide with questions and curiosity. "What are you doing here, Clive?"

"I told you I've come to take you home."

"I am home."

"Then I've come to drag you back where you belong and claim the artwork that belongs to me."

"I'm not interested. Have a nice life."

He took a step closer and grasped her wrist, squeezing tight enough that she gasped. "You don't want to fuck with me right now, Marnie. I fucking *own* you. And I don't give a shit what you want or where this smart-ass attitude has come from. I don't care if I have to walk in there and rip every picture off the wall. They're *mine*."

Black dots danced in front of Marnie's eyes as he squeezed her wrist harder. It had been a long time since she'd felt pain like that, and her knees started to buckle.

"You're going to want to let her go," Beckett said from somewhere behind her. "And you're going to want to do it right now."

She would've cried out in relief if she hadn't hurt so bad.

Clive looked over her shoulder and said, "This is none of your concern, cowboy. This is between me and my fiancé."

"I don't care who you say she is. You're not treating any woman like that. Now let her go or I'll make you."

Clive let go of her wrist and she sucked in a deep breath, cradling her hand to her stomach. She leaned against the wall and waited for the nausea to pass. Doors to the shops had started to open and people were gathering on the sidewalks to watch.

"What's going on, Beckett?" Cooper asked, coming out of the sheriff's office.

"I've got it under control. Mr. Wallace was just leaving."

"Know who I am, do you, cowboy?" Clive asked. "Then you know I'm nobody to fuck with. Especially not when it comes to my property. And this bitch is my property. Signed, sealed, and delivered in the contract. Marnie Whitlock is a household name in the world of photography. People pay hundreds of thousands of dollars for an original Marnie Whitlock. But everyone knows that artists are terrible at managing their money and their brand. Every picture hanging on that wall in that studio belongs to me. Hell, technically the studio should belong to me too because that's a business interest, and it says in our contract that I'm the sole executor of all of her business interests."

"Why don't you tell them how you drew the papers up without my knowledge and forced your secretary to sign my name, and then had one of your golfing buddy's file the paperwork?"

"Prove it," he said smugly. "Who's going to believe a piece of trash from the wrong side of the tracks? You can't fight a battle with me and win, Marnie."

"She might not be able to fight it by herself," Beckett said. "But there are plenty of people to help her. Do you want this fixed, Marnie? Just say the word."

"Yes," she said. It was time to stop running. To stop hiding.

Someone like Clive would never go away for long. And she was stronger than she'd once been. She'd made her life and her career, and what she chose to do with it was her decision alone. "I want my life back. He's not going to have power over me anymore."

Clive laughed and looked at her with malice in his eyes. "Now, sweetheart. We're going to get married. That'll seal everything up nice and tight. You know there's no use in resisting. I'm a man who always gets what he wants."

"Not this time," Beckett said.

"Listen, cowboy. I don't know who the hell you are, but if you want to keep your job so you can keep a roof over your head, I suggest you move along."

"I'm the head cowboy, and the ranch, the house, and a good part of the land you see belongs to me. You don't intimidate me."

Clive took a step forward. And then another. Until he was nose to nose with Beckett. But Beckett stood his ground. "Then maybe you should worry about being able to do business in any of the fifty states again. I'm a powerful man with powerful friends. In fact, the governor of your state happens to be one. I will crush you like a bug."

Clive kept his eye on Beckett, but he spoke to Marnie. "Start getting your things together. We're leaving tonight."

"You're out of your damned mind. What didn't you understand about no?" Marnie asked. "No, no, no. I'm not going. You don't own me. And I am going to fight you every step of the way, so unless you resort to kidnapping, I suggest you be the one to move along."

Clive spun around and his arm reached out to grab her, but Beckett had him on his knees with his arm pulled high behind his back in an instant.

"Lord, you must be hard of hearing," Beckett said. He pulled out his cell phone and made a call, and when the voice on the other end of the phone answered he breathed a sigh of relief.

"Uncle Jack," Beckett said. "I've got a man here who says he's a good friend of yours. Clive Wallace. Say hi, Clive."

Beckett put the phone up to Clive's ear and then pulled the arm behind his back up higher, making him squeal into the phone. Beckett took the phone back and then proceeded to explain everything that had transpired, mentioned forged signatures, fraud, and threats. Since Uncle Jack and the governor of Montana were one and the same, it helped to get as much of the story out as possible.

"You hear that, Clive? Jack's getting on the phone right now to *his* good friends, who are going to look into your business practices. He doesn't like the fact that you hurt the woman I love and plan on marrying."

Beckett paused as his uncle said something. "No, Uncle Jack. I haven't asked her yet. She's a prickly thing and stubborn too." He paused again. "Yep, just like Mama and Aunt Sarah. She'll fit right in."

Marnie sank down to the sidewalk and put her head between her knees. Everyone's emotions were hitting her at once, and she was hurting and too tired to block them. Marriage. Beckett wanted to marry her.

"You all right, Marnie?" Beckett asked. "Just take nice slow breaths. Do you think your wrist is broken?"

"It's fine," she said. "I'm more shocked that you actually want to marry me."

"Can y'all speak up?" someone yelled from across the street. "It's real hard to hear all the way over here."

"Of course I want to marry you," Beckett said. "I told you I love you. I want to spend my life with you. I've always wanted that. You're the only woman for me. You just needed to find your way back home. And look, here you are."

Clive struggled again and Beckett put the phone back to his ear when he remembered his uncle. "Sorry about that, Uncle Jack. I'm going to let you go now. Thanks for the help." He hung up the phone and bent down to whisper to Clive. "I have to tell you, I'm pretty sure you're going to owe Marnie a lot of money by the time they finish going through all your financial records. And I think Uncle Jack mentioned something about the IRS as well. That's going to be a bummer."

"You son of a bitch," Clive said, trying to twist out of his grasp.

"Nope, my mama's a real nice woman. Though she'd chew you up and spit you out. You're nothing but a chicken shit, preying on others you deem weaker and taking advantage of them. You picked the wrong person this time. Marnie had the strength to leave you in the first place, and you didn't bother to get to know her at all if you think she could've been persuaded to stay by the promise of money and fame. And you really don't know her at all if you think threats are going to work any better. She's survived a lot worse than you."

He pulled Clive to his feet but didn't let go of him. "Cooper, if you wouldn't mind taking him off my hands I need to go say a few words to the love of my life."

"What he'd say?" someone across the street yelled. "Toil and strife?"

"I'll take it from here," Cooper said, getting a good grip on Clive's arm. "Why don't we head to my office and have a chat about how to treat women?"

Beckett went to Marnie and knelt down beside her, gathering her gingerly in his arms.

"Let me love you, Marnie," he whispered against her hair. "You're so worth it."

A sob caught in her throat and she tightened her arms around his neck. He didn't care that they were in public or that an audience had gathered. As far as he was concerned it was just the two of them.

"I've loved you for so long," she said. "I never thought I deserved someone like you. Never expected you'd be mine when I finally came home. I've wanted to say it for so long, but I was afraid. I couldn't see our future when I tried to look. I could see everyone else's. But not ours. It terrified me to think of what that meant."

"Look in my eyes and you can see all the future you need, baby. I will never stop loving you."

When she finally met his gaze he saw his reflection in her eyes. "From this point forward," he said, "our future is the only thing that matters. The past is the past. The hurt and anger. Everything you survived, it made you who you are today. That's the woman I love. The woman I want to spend eternity with. Marry me, Marnie. Let me love you."

Her fingers twined in his hair and hope filled her eyes. "Be my future, Beckett. I love you too."

Epilogue

Five Months Later…

The MacKenzies knew how to throw a wedding. They'd had plenty of practice.

And Mary MacKenzie couldn't have asked for a more perfect day for the daughter of her heart to marry the man she loved. May in Montana was beautiful. The air was crisp and clear and everything was green.

Beckett and Marnie were married down by the water, standing beneath an arch of white flowers as they pledged to love and honor each other for eternity. Her dark hair shone against the lacy veil and her voice was clear as she said her vows.

It wasn't often the whole family was together in one place, but when they were, Mary's heart filled so much she thought it would burst. Even Shane had put on his suit and sat at the end of the row in his wheelchair, his pants leg pinned below the knee.

Shane's time was coming. If he didn't have faith in himself then she'd just have to have enough for the both of them. And she wasn't the only one who had faith in Shane. Doctor Lacy Shaw wasn't going to let him quit. That girl had a lot of fight in her. And Shane might not realize it, but even Mary could see the sparks between them.

He so reminded her of her first husband. But though she'd lost him young, she had no regrets. Because her love for Shane had been the love of youth. What she had with James was so much richer—deeper. They'd shared children, heartache, struggle, good times, and grandchildren. And she looked forward to waking next to him every morning and seeing what adventures were still in store for them.

She'd watched her children and her nephews find their mates through the years, and all she'd ever wanted for them was to find someone to give them the kind of fulfillment she and James gave each other. Nothing made her prouder than knowing her children had each picked someone who made them better—made them complete.

She still had one son who was unattached, and she had a feeling it wouldn't be long before her youngest began to heal. Losing a limb was something she could never imagine, and he'd been yanked from everything he'd ever known. He'd lost his command and been discharged from the Navy, and now he was floundering, wondering what kind of man he could ever hope to be.

But there was hope in healing. And when he healed and opened his heart, she had a feeling he'd find what he'd been missing all along.

The End

Sign up for the 1001 Dark Nights Newsletter
and be entered to win a Tiffany Lock necklace.

There's a contest every quarter!

Go to www.1001DarkNights.com to subscribe.

Discover the Liliana Hart
MacKenzie Family Collection

Rush
A MacKenzie Family Novella
by Robin Covington

From Liliana Hart's New York Times bestselling MacKenzie family comes a new story by USA Today bestselling author Robin Covington...

Atticus Rush doesn't really like people. Years in Special Ops and law enforcement showed him the worst of humanity, making his mountain hideaway the ideal place to live. But when his colleagues at MacKenzie Security need him to save the kidnapped young daughter of a U.S. Senator, he'll do it, even if it means working with the woman who broke his heart …his ex-wife.

Lady Olivia Rutledge-Cairn likes to steal things. Raised with a silver spoon and the glass slipper she spent years cultivating a cadre of acquaintances in the highest places. She parlayed her natural gift for theft into a career of locating and illegally retrieving hard-to-find items of value for the ridiculously wealthy. Rush was the one man who tempted her to change her ways…until he caught her and threatened to turn her in.

MacKenzie Security has vowed to save the girl. Olivia can find anything or anyone. Rush can get anyone out. As the clock winds down on the girl's life, can they fight the past, a ruthless madman and their explosive passion to get the job done?

* * * *

Bullet Proof
A MacKenzie Family Novella
by Avery Flynn

"Being one of the good guys is not my thing."

Bianca Sutherland isn't at an exclusive Eyes-Wide-Shut style orgy for the orgasms. She's there because the only clue to her friend's disappearance is a photo of a painting hanging somewhere in Bisu Manor. Determined to find her missing friend when no one else will, she expects trouble when she cons her way into the party—but not in the form of a so-hot-he-turns-your-panties-to-ash former boxer.

Taz Hazard's only concern is looking out for himself and he has no intention of changing his ways until he finds sexy-as-sin Bianca at the most notorious mansion in Ft. Worth. Now, he's tangled up in a missing person case tied into a powerful new drug about to flood the streets, if they can't find a way to stop it before its too late. Taking on a drug cartel isn't safe, but when passion ignites between them Taz and Bianca discover their hearts aren't bulletproof either.

* * * *

Delta: Rescue
A MacKenzie Family Novella
by Cristin Harber

When Luke Brenner takes an off-the-books job on the MacKenzie-Delta joint task force, he has one goal: shut down sex traffickers on his personal hunt for retribution. This operation brings him closer than he's ever been to avenge his first love, who was taken, sold, and likely dead.

Madeleine Mercier is the daughter of an infamous cartel conglomerate. Their family bleeds money, they sell pleasure, they sell people. She knows no other life, sees no escape, except for one.

Maddy is the only person who can take down Papa, when every branch of law enforcement in every country, is on her father's payroll.

It's evil. To want to ruin, to murder, her family. But that's what she is. Ruined for a life outside of destroying her father. She can't feel arousal. Has never been kissed. Never felt anything other than disgust for the world that she perpetuates. Until she clashes with a possible mercenary who gives her hope.

The hunter versus the virgin. The predator and his prey. When forced together, can enemies resist the urge to run away or destroy one another?

* * * *

Deep Trouble
A MacKenzie Family Novella
by Kimberly Kincaid

Bartender Kylie Walker went into the basement of The Corner Tavern for a box of cocktail napkins, but what she got was an eyeful of murder. Now she's on the run from a killer with connections, and one wrong step could be her last. Desperate to stay safe, Kylie calls the only person she trusts—her ex-Army Ranger brother. The only problem? He's two thousand miles away, and trouble is right outside her door.

Security specialist Devon Randolph might be rough and gruff, but he'll never turn down a friend in need, especially when that friend is the fellow Ranger who once saved his life. Devon may have secrets, but he's nearby, and he's got the skills to keep his buddy's sister safe...even if one look at brash, beautiful, Kylie makes him want to break all the rules.

Forced on the run, Kylie and Devon dodge bullets and bad guys, but they cannot fight the attraction burning between them.

Yet the closer they grow, the higher the stakes become. Will they be able to outrun a brutal killer? Or will Devon's secrets tear them apart first?

* * * *

Desire & Ice
A MacKenzie Family Novella
by Christopher Rice

Danny Patterson isn't a teenager anymore. He's the newest and youngest sheriff's deputy in Surrender, Montana. A chance encounter with his former schoolteacher on the eve of the biggest snowstorm to hit Surrender in years shows him that some schoolboy crushes never fade. Sometimes they mature into grown-up desire.

It's been years since Eliza Brightwell set foot in Surrender. So why is she back now? And why does she seem like she's running from something? To solve this mystery, Danny disobeys a direct order from Sheriff Cooper MacKenzie and sets out into a fierce blizzard, where his courage and his desire might be the only things capable of saving Eliza from a dark force out of her own past.

1001 Dark Nights

Welcome to 1001 Dark Nights… a collection of novellas that are breathtakingly sexy and magically romantic. Some are paranormal, some are erotic. Each and every one is compelling and page turning.

Inspired by the exotic tales of The Arabian Nights, 1001 Dark Nights features *New York Times* and *USA Today* bestselling authors.

In the original, Scheherazade desperately attempts to entertain her husband, the King of Persia, with nightly stories so that he will postpone her execution.

In our versions, month after month, each of our fabulous authors puts a unique spin on the premise and creates a tale that a new Scheherazade tells long into the dark, dark night.

For more information, visit www.1001DarkNights.com

About Liliana Hart

Liliana Hart is a *New York Times*, *USA Today*, and Publisher's Weekly Bestselling Author of more than 40 titles. After starting her first novel her freshman year of college, she immediately became addicted to writing and knew she'd found what she was meant to do with her life. She has no idea why she majored in music.

Since self-publishing in June of 2011, Liliana has sold more than 4 million ebooks and been translated into eight languages. She's appeared at #1 on lists all over the world and all three of her series have appeared on the New York Times list. Liliana is a sought after speaker and she's given keynote speeches and self-publishing workshops to standing-room-only crowds from California to New York to London.

Liliana can almost always be found at her computer writing or on the road giving workshops for SilverHart International, a company she founded with her husband, Scott Silverii, where they provide law enforcement, military, and fire resources for writers so they can write it right. Liliana is a recent transplant to Southern Louisiana, where she's getting used to the humidity and hurricane season, and plotting murders (for her books, of course).

Connect with me online:
twitter.com/Liliana_Hart
facebook.com/LilianaHart
My Website: www.lilianahart.com

Whiskey on the Rocks

Addison Holmes Mysteries
By Liliana Hart
Part of the Red Sole Clues Anthology
Coming March 22, 2016

I've seen a lot of male genitalia in my life.

Okay, maybe not a lot. But I've seen a few in real life, and I might have seen one or two in a dirty movie Nick and I rented a few months back. I wasn't impressed by the movie genitalia. All I could think was that those poor girls must get a lot of urinary tract infections.

And if I'm being honest, male genitalia is not the most attractive thing on the planet, even when it belongs to someone like Nick, who has very impressive attributes and knows just what to do with them. I've always thought male dangly bits looked something along the lines of a forlorn Snuffaluffagus—a little sad, a droopy trunk, and tufts of hair sprouting from every which direction.

My name is Addison Holmes, and there's a reason genitalia is at the forefront of my mind. I'm a private investigator at the McClean Detective Agency. By the grace of God and hot fudge sundaes, I'd somehow managed to pass all portions of the exam that allowed me to carry the laminated license with my photo on it, as well as the pink-handled 9mm I kept in my Kate Spade handbag. I'd bought the Glock and the handbag out of the trunk of Louis Bergman's Cadillac when I'd gone home to Whiskey Bayou for the holidays. He'd been running a two-for-one special.

A fat lot of good the handbag and Glock were doing me now though. It would look a little foolish to be carrying an almost genuine Kate Spade around a nudist colony, and carrying concealed wasn't really an option. The best I could do was hide my Glock under a towel in the beach bag I carried.

I was uncomfortable enough standing on the pier in the buff with Rosemarie and Aunt Scarlet at my side. A three-thousand dollar camera hung around my neck, leaving a very interesting tan line down the center of each of my boobs from the strap. I'd been pretending to take pictures of seagulls for the last fifteen minutes, when in fact, I was trying to take pictures of Elmer Hughes, a man whose Snuffaluffagus was approximately a hundred years old and looked like it suffered from elephantiasis.

"Lord, would you look at the testicles on that man," Aunt Scarlet said. "They're the size of oranges. How do you think he keeps from sitting on them?"

"You think he's had implants?" Rosemarie asked. "I've heard plastic surgeons down here make a killing on senior citizens. People get to a certain age and then want to discover the fountain of youth."

"And testicular implants are supposed to make you look younger?" I asked skeptically, trying to zoom in on Elmer.

"Everything droops when you get to be my age," Scarlet said. "We always associate tighter with youthfulness. Instead of getting the implants, he should've given those puppies a facelift. They almost hang all the way to his knees."

Elmer was down on the beach under one of the umbrellas, sunning on a lounger topside up, making sure his oranges got plenty of sun. I could barely get a decent shot of the tattoo on his arm, and even with the full zoom and focus of the camera, it was still difficult to make out. Age hadn't been kind to Elmer Hughes.

"I thought about getting my lady parts tightened up a bit," Scarlet continued. "They call it vaginal rejuvenation, if you can believe that. I haven't had anything rejuvenating down there since the time I walked through Wally Pinkerton's yard and all the sprinklers came on."

"Umm—" I said, for lack of anything better.

"I was going to get rejuvenated because a couple of years ago I thought I might be getting some action, and I wanted everything to look as if it just came out of the factory. But the fellow up and died on me before we could get all hot and bothered. Take my advice, Addison. Never let a man die when they're laying on top of you. Thank God he was wearing one of those medic alert buttons around his neck, because I never would've been able to push him off to reach the phone."

I was in a complete state of Zen. Or it could have been the Xanax I'd taken with my mojito at lunch. There was no other way to survive being naked with two people I had no desire to be naked with, or listen to the conversation we were currently having without it.

"It's probably best you opted out of the surgery," Rosemarie said. "Sharon Osbourne said it was excruciating."

"Ehh, I don't have much feeling left down there anyway," Scarlet said with a shrug. "I've stopped holding out hope."

"You've just got to wait for a man who's big enough to make things seem not so loosey goosey down there."

Since Scarlet had just celebrated her ninetieth, I was thinking finding that particular man might be a challenge.

"I'm going to have to get closer," I said, hoping this would distract them from the conversation.

"Look," Rosemarie said. "Those loungers right next to him just came open. Lets get them before someone else does. You should be able to take plenty of pictures from that angle."

I sighed and let go of the camera so it hung around my neck. I wanted to say there was something freeing about standing completely naked on the pier, the wind tousling my hair and the sun beating down on my bare skin, but I'd be lying. I pretty much felt just like I had during middle school—awkward posture due to not knowing what to do with my body, awkward hair that frizzed in humidity no matter how much I straightened it, and awkward friends that pretty much guaranteed a lot of time standing next to the punch bowl at school dances.

I'd had my nether regions freshly waxed for this occasion and my body was still in pretty good shape from back when I'd passed the physical fitness portion of my P.I. exam. I maintained the physique by doing hot yoga one day a week and occasionally watching a Jillian Michael's DVD from the couch. She scared the crap out of me. My butt cheeks clenched every time she screamed at someone that unless they were going to puke, faint, or die then they should keep going. My butt was really starting to look good.

"I still don't understand how you could recognize the tattoo," I said to Scarlet. "It's so wrinkled and distorted it's nearly impossible to make out."

"Some things you don't forget," she said sagely. "The Savannah bank robbery of '45 and a Latin lover named Mario are the two things that stick with me the most. Whew, was your Uncle

Stan steamed about Mario. But once I explained he was Spanish Royalty and it was an honor to be asked to sleep with him, Stan calmed right down." She looked confused for a minute and slapped her hand on top of her head to keep her hat from blowing away. "May he rest in peace."

Rosemarie and I stared at Scarlet with horrified fascination, and I did a half-assed sign of the cross along with Rosemarie and Scarlet at the mention of Uncle Stanley's untimely demise. I was mostly Methodist, so I was never really sure if I was crossing myself correctly, but no one had made devil horn signs at me or doused me with holy water, so I figured I was in the clear.

We made our way back to the stairs that led down to the beach and I dug my flip-flops out of the bag so the sand wouldn't burn my feet. I looked like an idiot wearing nothing but a camera and flip-flops, but to those at the Hidden Sunrise Naturist Community, I looked like I belonged.

We spread our towels out on the loungers, adjusted the umbrellas so we were protected from direct sunlight, and got comfortable. I set the camera on the little table next to the loungers and pointed it at Elmer, who seemed to be snoozing peacefully on the lounger a few feet away.

The problem with the camera was that it made noise when pictures were taken, and I didn't know how sound of a sleeper Elmer was. So I used my second best option and pulled out my iPhone.

The beach waiter came up and took our drink orders, and I sighed, frustrated, because I couldn't get a clear shot of the tattoo on his arm with my phone. I had to have the tattoo. It was the only documented proof the FBI had of The Romeo Bandit, aka, Elmer Hughes.

I watched Elmer for ten more minutes and contemplated my choices while I sipped on a Sex on the Beach. Rosemarie was reading a book two loungers over, and Aunt Scarlet had gotten bored and was building a sandcastle, wearing nothing but a big hat and a lot of sand she was probably going to regret getting up close and personal with later.

"Don't forget the sunscreen, Aunt Scarlet," I called out a little too loud, watching Elmer closely to see if he stirred. Nope. He was out for the count. It was now or never.

I took another fortifying sip of my drink and grabbed the camera. I put the camera strap around my neck and got on all fours in the hot sand. I might have muttered an expletive or two, having not thought through the fact that it would feel like dipping my hands and knees in molten glass.

I tried not to think about what I looked like from behind. And then I did think about it and grabbed the towel off my lounger, draping it across my backside like a tablecloth. I slowly crawled on hands and knees until I was inches away from Elmer Hughes.

My heart was pounding in my chest and I was covered with sweat and sand, neither of my favorite things. I realized I had a slight buzz and the Xanax must have worn off because I was feeling a whole lot of anxiety all of a sudden.

Elmer let out a soft snore and I squeaked. His arm was limp and his hands were gnarled with age. He wore a pinky ring with a small ruby in the center. The tattoo was wrinkled and the ink had faded over the years, but now that I was up close, I could see it clearly. A thorny vine and rosary beads were twined around a naked woman that had more curves than Kim Kardashian. The vine and the rosary beads ended at the top of his hand where the rose had started to bloom.

I could see how in its heyday the tattoo might have been an interesting conversation piece, but the inked woman was now wizened with age and arm hair, and it looked vaguely as if she were shooting the rosary out of her vagina. But Aunt Scarlet had recognized it, and that was all that mattered.

I brought the camera up and took a couple of quick shots, and then I bit my lip as I debated whether or not to stretch his skin out a little and get a more complete picture. I finally decided that was the alcohol talking and probably not the best decision, and then I realized the alcohol had been giving me direction through this whole debacle because what I was doing definitely wasn't using my best judgment.

I found this out the hard way when I turned to crawl back to my own lounger and my towel got stuck under my knee, pulling it completely off and leaving me bare-assed with my lady bits flapping in the breeze.

"Yikes," a male voice said behind me.

I scrambled to cover my rear with the towel and turned my head in time to catch Elmer Hughes horrified stare.

"Jesus God," he wheezed, clutching his chest. "I thought I was having a flashback from the seventies. Those things looked a lot different then. Nothing like 70's bush. You've got a nice landscaper."

I turned fifty shades of red and scrambled to make sure I was completely covered with the towel. And then I noticed his gaze had shifted to the camera in my hand.

"I can explain," I said.

On behalf of 1001 Dark Nights,

Liz Berry and M.J. Rose would like to thank ~

Liliana Hart
Scott Silverii
Steve Berry
Doug Scofield
Kim Guidroz
Jillian Stein
InkSlinger PR
Asha Hossain
Kasi Alexander
Chris Graham
Pamela Jamison
Jessica Johns
Dylan Stockton
and Simon Lipskar

Printed in Great Britain
by Amazon